THE MYTH OF JUNE

THE MYTH OF JUNE

THE VIOLENTS BOOK ONE

A. B. DANIELS-ANNACHI

Potential Triggers: Death, Domestic Abuse, Kidnapping/Hostage of Adult, Gun Violence, Mention of Alcohol, Murder, Pregnancy, Sexism, Sexual Assault, Violence

To my readers — Welcome to the universe; I hope you enjoy your stay.

And Poseidon . . . maybe if you weren't such a dick, I wouldn't have had to write this book.

1

Typhon hovered above a wilted cactus and shook his head at the webs of disease stretching around its spines. As if the black lines that arced and wove through the plant, cracking its tender flesh, weren't a signal enough that something was wrong, a pale liquid oozed from its surface. The drops fell to the desert sand below and sent the veins of sick racing after themselves through the rest of the plains.

He looked around the plant again—it stood the height of a mortal man, maybe meeting his shin, and had long, thick needles poking out at odd angles. Its outer skin was a cool shade of dark green, akin to a fully grown dryad.

"What's happened to you?" he whispered to the crown of the cactus.

When it didn't respond, he rode his breeze higher, dispersing himself around the

1

sky above the cracking ground of the Tabernas Desert, and pondered how to tackle the problem. On one hand, Zeus disliked any darkness plaguing his mortal realm—his creation. On the other hand, perhaps this had occurred naturally and should be left alone. But how could a cactus create such sickness in itself that it rots out half a desert?

He wove higher, scanning the area and following the path of veins. As far as he could see, they tucked underground from plant to plant, eating each bundle of roots. Near the outer third of the plains, the plant life thinned, and the rot might stop itself. But just beyond, near the northern border, sat a thick forest, ripe for consumption.

He spun a loop toward the treetops, dragging a plume of sand on his trail.

If any mortal happened to be venturing through the desert, it may appear there was a large dust devil turning about in an untoward fashion, weaving and skipping around rocks and plants. But to Typhon, he was just bobbing around to the sound of a symphony in his mind.

The jungle started sparsely but grew quite dense only a few dozen yards in, with trees as thick as an Olympic column and vines woven tight enough to block the forest floor from the late evening sunlight. He considered trying to squeeze between the canopy branches but didn't want his winds to disturb any of the potential life there, so he coasted above instead, rustling leaves here and there.

As he flew, his admiration for the lush greenery began to turn to dread as he looked back at the veining in the sand. It wasn't far off—maybe a few days of growth away. Then who knew what would happen to the trees.

He slowed his winds. Priapus would know. Now that he thought of it, the God of Gardens had potentially grown this forest, or even started the rot that was going to kill it.

He had the brief thought that perhaps he needn't intervene with what was happening at all, perhaps it was one of the other gods' work to begin with.

But as he flew further north and cleared the forest's canopy, the thought dissipated faster than his essence in the wind. For just before him lay the greatest mortal city he'd ever seen.

Great spiraling towers were posted at each cardinal point outside the city, holding steadfast adobe walls. Typhon's jaw dropped at the depth of the walls, how they held walkways ten men wide, and he flew toward the city and gasped.

The inside of the borders protecting the grand city were carved with an irrigation system. Water sloshed from the top of the towers down pipes that were open to the sky. He followed the racing streams as they separated into curves and sharp angles through expansive fields that stretched between the walls and the first cottages of the city. Some pipes stopped at wells, and how they didn't overflow without the aid of some magic, he wasn't sure. Other pipes tapered off to a closed style with many holes in it, allowing the water to seep out slowly into the fields.

Beyond the ring of small houses stood larger buildings, with well-engineered roads between them. People dressed in loosely draped clothes milled about, some on foot, while others climbed into what looked like horseless carriages that spewed smoke and moved faster, too.

Typhon wove through the city on his breeze, twisting around spires and drifting through windows. The towers only grew in size and grandeur as he found the middle of the city, where a lone squat building sat, reminiscent of a temple. It was surrounded by gardens on all sides, and more residents had gathered in its grasses. They knelt among the flowers with their heads tipped to the sun and uttered prayers for relief from the rot.

Typhon's stomach sank as he understood that they knew what was coming. He had to go to Zeus for a solution. If the sickness creeping its way through the earth reached this civilization, who knew what they would lose.

He spun up into the wind and let his essence shift through the seam between realms. A glimpse of bright light passed him in a flash before he stood in front of the columns of Olympus' front gate.

He strode through the arch quickly, cutting past a small group of Olympians huddled near one of the main support pillars of the great room. It didn't take long to find Zeus, his form towering over everyone else. He must have just come from a mission, as he still stood in his Olympic form—all purple skin arced with white traces of lightning and eyes full of a swirling storm.

"Zeus!" Typhon called out to the god's back, and immediately regretted it, as he saw what he was walking into.

Zeus turned to reveal Hades and Ares standing behind a small conference table. Both had their arms crossed, and Hades looked as if someone had just spat on his sandals.

"You better not have been attacked too. We need to deal with my domain first," Hades said, anger tainting his voice.

Ares shifted uncomfortably, and Zeus brushed his silvery hair back, beginning to shrink down to the same height as the other Olympians around.

"What's going on?" Typhon asked as he approached the end of the table.

"Underworld was attacked again. I can only imagine that it was the same perpetrator as last time," Hades scoffed.

"But we also don't know for sure. Nothing was stolen. They didn't make it through the gateway, thanks to Cerberus," Ares finished.

Hades beamed at the mention of his newest pet. Typhon raised a brow and looked to Zeus. Underworld was the domain that Hades looked over, and, save for the rivers that ran through it, it was very much the mirror of Olympus as Hades was to Zeus. The last time it had been invaded was during the Titan's War. He understood what a big deal this was to the gods, but as a titan, he couldn't quite fathom the overt concern if no damage was done.

"What do you need?" Zeus asked.

"Right." He looked around the group, still uncomfortable. Though he was older than all of them, he held no power here and disliked bringing issues to the Ruler of Gods. "There is a disease in a desert, outside of a civilization in the mortal realm. It will reach them soon, perhaps within the year. I'm unsure if the rot was caused by another Olympian, if it's fated, or if it's a natural occurrence—"

"Destroy the desert," Zeus said with a wave of his hand.

"Happily. But the people, I worry about what they may do when encountered with such a storm."

"I said what I said." He turned his clouded gray eyes on Typhon and held his gaze. "The people, if meant to survive, will do so. If you hold concern for the rot, then destroy it. Otherwise, if you care to find its source, by all means, seek out Priapus or try and find Asclepius." The look of disgust on his face told Typhon that he really didn't want that.

Typhon nodded slowly. "They have great technology, Zeus. I don't want something to go—"

"Would you disobey me?"

"No," Typhon answered quickly.

"Then, destroy it," Zeus said firmly.

Typhon hesitated, thinking about the hundreds of robed mortals knelt around their temple before he nodded and turned from the group. He caught the whispered name "Poseidon" thrown between the trio before he shifted through the arch, toward the desert once more.

As he thought of Poseidon and wove through that sliver of blank space between the realms, he was yanked to the side, and his feet landed on a hard-packed dirt road instead of in soft sand. A red brick manor stood in front of him, surrounded by sprawling hills on all sides.

Typhon looked around the fields for an inkling of where he was before he strode toward the stairs and lifted the brass knocker. Its clanging sound echoed behind the heavy door once, twice, thrice, with no answer. This definitely was not the desert, and it seemed no one was home to greet him anyway. Why had his shift brought him here?

After a few moments, he pushed his way into the house and called out.

"Hello?"

The foyer was empty, but the many heavy paintings and rugs scattered about the room absorbed his call. The back of his neck bristled as he headed toward an open door on his right. Before he could venture any further into the house, two voices met his ears, and a moment later, Poseidon emerged in front of him.

Typhon crossed his arms and raised a brow. Last time he'd seen the God of the Sea, Poseidon had been narrowly escaping a mortal law enforcer. Not living in a rich estate.

"Typhon!" his voice boomed. "Welcome, Uncle. What can I do for you?"

"I've just been to see Zeus," Typhon started. He noticed a flicker of annoyance cross Poseidon's face and wondered if perhaps he had a purpose in turning up here. A beat passed between them before he asked, "How has it been lately?" He was referring to the tension constantly building between the brothers, but something told him that there was more going on in the younger god's life.

"Fine—normal. He still threatens to banish me. I have been attending to my own matters," Poseidon said stiffly.

"I have an assignment," Typhon said, lifting a hand, and Poseidon shook his head.

"Count me out," Poseidon spoke before Typhon could continue.

Typhon tapped his chin and shifted on the balls of his feet. "Perhaps if you assisted with this storm—"

"I should not have to keep trying to win his favor," he cut off Typhon. "There is no reason for his behavior, or his standing."

Typhon froze. He hadn't seen Poseidon so vehemently against Zeus before. Sure, they had disagreements, but to insinuate that the ruler of Olympus shouldn't be in charge . . . There must be some greater strife that he was unaware of.

"Poseidon, in an effort to keep peace among the Council, and perhaps further your standing in his eyes, you might consider accompanying me on my quest." Typhon fixed him with a serious look.

Poseidon finally sighed. "I suppose you're right. It might distract from any other issues he may take with me in the future."

Typhon raised a brow but didn't comment further. He nodded and jerked a thumb over his shoulder. "I'll meet you there. Southern Tabernas, just west of the sea."

The younger god nodded and waved a hand over his shoulder as he turned back to the hallway. A shuffling reached Typhon's ears, and the hair on the back of his neck pricked. He strained his eyes for only a moment before Poseidon's broad back shielded his view and lost any chance of seeing who might be lurking in the shadows.

He flew over the ocean, his essence spreading out wide over the waves to sweep up stray droplets of sea spray as he coasted in the wind. Poseidon appeared underneath him only a few moments later, raising waves taller than the pillars of Olympus. Water and wind spun around them, rising into the sky and turning outward as Typhon flew, until he held the eye of a hurricane.

The downpour pelted the rotting sands, washing diseased plants away and tearing their roots to shreds before his eyes. Typhon's heart leapt as he watched pieces of sick leaves and cactus stems get caught in his waves to be sifted away from the healthy part of the forest. As he approached the thick of the trees, where he could see the edge of the city from, he began to slow his winds.

"What are you doing?" Poseidon called up to him.

"The rot only lies in the sands," Typhon replied, pulling hard against his own rains.

Poseidon turned his torrent further toward the city and lifted high above the treetops. "I see the people there, Typhon. Their architecture resembles our own, and they have vehicles far more technical than any other. Are they not the disease?"

"No," Typhon said. "I don't know why their civilization has moved so far ahead, but we cannot punish them for it."

"What is this place called?" asked Poseidon.

"They call themselves Atlantis," Typhon replied, awe in his voice. "I think they will pave the way for the rest of the world through their creativity."

A beat passed before Poseidon tore his part of their storm away.

"What are you doing?" Typhon screamed above the crash of thunder.

Poseidon turned back as he reached the tree line. "Don't you see that they are causing the rot? If left unchecked, they will become an unfair world power."

Typhon slowed. Was that possible? They had amazing, wonderful inventions just in their roads, their walls—surely they would use their advancements for good once they made travel connections with other places.

Poseidon was already moving. He called his waves in from the sea, throwing them high in the air, forcing the weather to co-operate and bend to his will. Typhon yelled above the storm, trying to take back control, but it was too late. He watched as their creation took a far more destructive turn than he intended, and, directed by Poseidon, it descended on the city.

Vegetation floated through the streets between buildings, followed by the pipes that had kept it alive. Bricks crumbled and fell, and shortly after, the people that had been hiding in their homes began to burst through their doors as well. Some were still alive and had made themselves rafts of various pieces of wood or window shuttering. Others were simply vacated bodies that joined the debris.

Typhon watched in horror as Poseidon slowly leveled the city, and as the buildings fell faster, the sand that the foundation had been laid on began to shift, and the earth quaked. Cracks ran under the ocean that encroached on their once beautiful civilization, and suddenly the water began draining.

Poseidon yelled in surprise and pulled up, hovering next to Typhon as the lower level that remained began to fall into the sand.

They watched together while the citizens scrambled to escape, and failed. The rain poured and the sea drained, falling through hidden caverns where the roads had been, along with the remnants of buildings.

Suddenly the desert was quiet. All that remained of the city was a small amount of debris and a single spire sticking up from the sand.

300
YEARS LATER

2

June wiped the sweat from her palms on her dress and took a deep breath to calm her nerves. The bellowing voice from across the field of chairs did nothing for her anxiety, so she turned back to her family's conversation.

"I just don't understand why we're outside for the ceremony this year. Last year's graduating class was inside," her father grumbled.

"This class is much larger, William. A lot of people move to Manhattan every day," Ty said, raising a thick brow. "The world is in unrest. People are struggling."

A nerve in William's stubbled jaw twitched, but he didn't say anything further.

"How has work been? Has anything new happened at the plant?" Ty asked.

William's shoulders tensed, and he looked around and wrung his hands. "Fine, why would anything happen? Have you heard of something?"

"No, I'm just making small talk. I haven't seen you in a while."

Ty looked at June helplessly, and she shrugged. There was nothing she could do to intervene—while her father was prone to moods, Ty was nothing but logical, which made William angrier.

"Nothing. Never mind," Ty sighed, and brushed a hand through his fiery red hair, pushing the bits down that stuck up. He turned to June and asked, "Are you excited for the ceremony?"

She smiled. "Yeah, it'll be nice to have it done with. I'm ready to move on and really get going with my art." She grinned and looked at her mother. Helen was an artist as well—she had been painting long before June was born and had inspired the first of June's pieces.

Though Helen nodded along, her deep-green eyes were distant. June reached out and slipped a hand through her mother's. The older woman squeezed her fingers before pointing at a few other families filing in.

"Should we take our seats?" she asked, nearly too quiet to hear.

"Yeah, I should join my class," June said.

William stomped off toward the bleachers, and Ty grimaced before offering his arm to Helen. "Good luck, June-Bee." He winked as he led her mother away.

June shook her head and made her way toward the seats set out for the graduating class. Parents—or other family and friends, like Ty—would sit far across the field. Though they came to support her as she earned her diploma, she was glad she wouldn't have to hear William snap at anyone, or strain to hear Helen's mumbling.

A few classmates waved, and she returned the gesture, but nearly tripped when she saw a tall figure jogging toward her. Sunlight glinted off their golden shirt as they turned around the path, scanning the crowd.

"Denny?" she called out and waved.

They raised a hand to shield their golden eyes and looked at her before jogging the rest of the way.

"Sorry I'm late. I had to close the restaurant, and there were a few stragglers." Their voice was smooth, even though they'd been running.

June waved her hand. "No matter, I didn't think you were coming. I had forgotten about work when I invited you."

Denny bent forward, having to tilt their head to meet her eyes on account of how tall they were, and patted her shoulder. "Of course I had to show up. I understand the relationship with your father is . . . rocky, at best. I may not be him, but I feel some sort of responsibility, being your boss and all."

She smiled, but before she could thank them, the principal called out that it was time for everyone to take a seat.

Denny shooed her away and strode toward the bleachers, and she fell into line behind the other 'G' last names before sitting.

"I'm honored to present your graduating class of nineteen twenty-six," a voice boomed over the field, and the buzzing of the crowd quieted. June exchanged a look with the girl next to her, who raised a brow as the speaker crackled.

The principal continued talking, sharing a speech about the greatness to come from the youth of this year, some more about what would come in their future. June nearly fell asleep at one point until the commencement finally began and names were called.

The lines moved quickly after that, starting with "Adams, Hannah" and continuing through the row in front of June's, which finished with "Holsted, Greg." Her row stood as one. Before she knew it, "Georgian, Juniper" was called, and she was marching across the makeshift stage to cheers from her family and scattered applause from her class.

Juniper shook the hand of her principal before accepting her diploma and walking back to her seat. Her class buzzed with excitement as there was one last round of congratulations from the administrators and they were released to their families.

June walked through the rows of seats quickly before she could be closed in. She found her family hovering just outside of the field, waiting for her.

"We're so proud of you!" Ty gushed.

"Look at you, you made it," cooed her mother, with tears in her eyes.

William patted her back and offered her a brief smile before turning to the walking path. "Shall we head to lunch?"

Juniper nodded and fell into step behind him, glancing back at the rest of her class, most of which were still milling about and celebrating. She caught the eye of her friend Barbara but continued shuffling toward her father's car. She would have liked to stay, but with how easily irritated he could get, she didn't want to ask. She looked around one last time. Even Denny had already left.

Her mother nudged her arm and smiled, and she returned the gesture.

The drive to Denny's diner was short. William didn't ask anyone if that's where they should eat, but announced as he shifted the car into park that he would enjoy a slice of pie to celebrate June's achievement.

She mumbled her agreement, and Ty stiffened in the seat next to her.

"What's wrong?" she asked in a hushed voice as they walked from the parking lot to the front door.

"Oh, you know I just don't like Denny all that much."

"Right. I forget why?" June asked.

Ty shrugged as he stepped away from the car, but didn't answer.

The bell on the handle jingled as William opened the door, and he turned to June. "Go and order for us. Just pie for the table," he commanded.

Helen cleared her throat quietly next to him, and he raised a brow at her. "I thought we were getting lunch, dear," she said.

"I just want pie," he retorted, voice firm.

"Yes, but the rest of us might be hungry." Her voice faltered as he glared at her. He pushed past instead of answering and led the way to a table in the back corner.

"Should I . . .?" June allowed her question to trail off as Helen patted her arm.

"Just the pie, dear."

June nodded and glanced around. When she didn't spot Denny in the busy crowd, she ducked behind the counter and grabbed an order pad herself, scribbling down the note and sticking the receipt in the window for Chef.

Nearly every table in the building was full, and she was sure that Denny was in the kitchen helping out. If they saw her, she'd likely get recruited to serve tables, which would push William over the edge.

She wove around chairs that were pulled out too far and dodged the waving arms of parents telling animated stories of their children before she found her seat by her mother. Ty was talking about something with Helen while William looked around anxiously.

"Are you okay, Dad?" June asked.

His head snapped to her, and he cleared his throat. "Yes. I just thought I saw a colleague from work. Is that order on its way?"

She nodded and looked to Ty, who reached across the table.

A calm feeling enveloped her, and she felt as if she were sitting in a cozy room during a storm as he patted the back of her hand. She relaxed back into her chair.

"So, what's next, June?" he asked.

"Well, I still need to grab the last of my things from Mom's house before school applications open. Denny gave me the key to the storage space yesterday, so I have a place to put all of my sculptures that are crowding Mom's studio. I can finally start fresh." She glanced at her mother as she spoke, anxious for Helen's reaction, but the older woman just made a humming sound and stared at the table, seeming oblivious to the conversation. Helen had been upset when June started the process of moving out two months prior, but she seemed to be unbothered now.

"That sounds great. Let me know if you need any help. I'm just down the road now," he said with a smile. He pulled his hand back and cleared his throat, reaching into his jacket. "I am so proud of you. I know I'm not exactly the same as a true uncle, but I feel lucky to have been around all these years. Watching you grow has truly been a privilege." Ty swiped a finger under an eye before producing a small box from the inner pocket of his jacket. "I wanted to give you a gift to mark this momentous occasion."

June grinned as she took the heavy case. The ribbon on top came undone easily, and inside on a bed of velvet lay a shining gold watch.

"To count down the hours until your name is known around the world," Ty said.

Before June could respond, William slapped a hand hard onto the tabletop and stood. All three turned to look at him in shock.

"What's wrong, Will?" Helen asked.

A nerve twitched in his forehead before he shook his head and looked around the diner. June followed his gaze over the busy tables, but didn't see anything out of the ordinary. The post-graduation crowd was buzzing, and Denny stood talking to a customer across the restaurant.

"I have to leave." He shuffled away from the table without looking at anyone.

Helen looked to Ty with a baffled expression, and his brows shot up.

"What was that? Where's he going?" June asked, rising to look through the restaurant, but William was already gone.

3

Helen stood frozen behind her dining chair. The smells of the chicken casserole and steamed vegetables she'd cooked wafted through the air, pulling a rumble from her stomach. As the minutes ticked by, her gaze remained fixed on her husband's empty seat. Six o'clock passed, then six-thirty. The smells faded, and the fizzing bubbles from their cider stopped popping through the air.

Something stirred in her mind, behind the veil of numbness that held her in place, waiting. Where was he? Dinner was at five-thirty every night. It wasn't like him to be late. At least, she didn't think so. A crease furrowed her brow as she tried to remember the last time she had asked where he had been for the day, or when they'd last had a conversation about how their days had gone. Helen looked at the clock again: seven-oh-five. She tapped her foot impatiently and snatched up her drink, draining it quickly before walking through the house.

"William?" she called.

No response came. She checked their room, the guest room, and even Juniper's vacated bedroom, but found no sign of her husband. How could he be so inconsiderate to be an hour and a half late for dinner?

As she approached his office, an anxious feeling settled into her stomach. She rapped on the door twice and held her breath, but no answer came. She knocked again, a bit harder, and looked at the door handle. She hadn't been in William's office in years. She wasn't sure she was even supposed to go in.

Her heart raced as she reached for the knob, and time seemed to slow. Anxiety churned her stomach as she wrapped her fingers around the cool metal.

Before she could twist the handle, the front door slammed and she jumped away, taking in a sharp breath. She bustled down the hall as fast as possible, skidding to a halt in the doorway as William was removing his shoes.

He looked up at her with a startled expression and asked, "What are you doing?"

"Nothing." The word flew from her mouth in a gasp. "Where were you?"

William's jaw twitched. "Don't worry about it. Is dinner ready?"

The anxiety that Helen had been feeling pulsed away into anger, and she swallowed hard. "Dinner was nearly two hours ago, Will."

His steps stuttered before he continued to the dining table. "Warm it up. I'm hungry."

"Warm it up? William, I've been waiting for you for two hours. Where were you?"

William stopped in front of his chair and turned to face her, the nerve above his brow pulsating. "That's none of your business."

"I think it is. You stormed from the diner this afternoon, leaving June at her celebration, then turned up late for dinner. I'm your wife, I think I deserve to know," Helen retorted.

She regretted snapping as William's face contorted in anger. He tightened his fists around the back of his chair. "Where I go is my business. Your job is to take care of the house. Correct?"

Helen's previous flood of emotion dissipated as the shroud of numbness fell back over her mind.

William strode toward her and grabbed her face, leaning down to fix his steely blue gaze on her wide eyes. "Do not ever question me and my whereabouts. You have your duty, I have mine. Understand?" His tone was seething, and fear settled into her bones. She nodded as much as his firm grip on her jaw would allow, and he released her with a jerk of his hand, moving to his seat and brushing away the stray pieces of hair that had fallen in front of his eyes. "Heat it up." He said the words low. She nodded again as she gathered their plates.

Out of view in the kitchen, she rubbed the sore spot where his thumb had pressed into her skin and watched his food on the stove, letting her mind go blank. It wasn't until the smells overwhelmed her that she moved again, silently placing his plate back in front of him.

He said nothing as she stood back. As his fork scraped the plate, she inched toward the front door.

Her feet guided her toward the sidewalk, and she found herself gasping against the brisk night air. Tears stung her cheeks, and she gripped her sweater closed at her throat to keep herself from sobbing. She turned at the corner, mindlessly walking down the road toward Ty's house, but quickly changed her path, instead taking a right, then left twice until she neared a park.

A bench greeted her, and Helen sat, sniffling, and pressed her face into her hands. As she worked to stifle her tears and calm herself, she heard the clack of shoes nearby.

She offered a small wave to the person strolling down the pavement toward her. "Hello, Denny."

They looked up and nodded in her direction, pulling their hat further over their slicked-back hair. Their short, sharp heels clacked louder as they sped up to meet her, and the end of their woven scarf flapped in the wind.

"Good evening, Helen. What are you doing out so late?" they asked.

Helen patted the bench next to her, inviting them to sit, before letting out a mangled sound that landed somewhere between a sigh and a laugh. "I needed a bit of an escape."

Denny raised a penciled brow as they crossed their ankles and looked her up and down. "Is everything okay at home?"

Helen nodded furiously. "Just dandy. I wanted a walk, is all."

"I know that our only connection is through Juniper, but you can talk to me. If there is a problem with William—"

"No, it's fine." Helen cut them off and brushed her hands down her skirt. When she turned back and caught their gaze lingering on her arms, she looked down and noticed the faded bruises on one wrist from an argument with Will the week before. She hastily pulled her sleeves farther down.

"How is June doing at work, anyway? The restaurant was busy when we stopped in earlier," Helen asked, waving off their concerned gaze.

Denny nodded. "She's been great. We'll only be busier as summer wears on."

"That's wonderful to hear. She's very grateful."

Denny hummed in response, and silence stretched between them as the moon rose in the sky and crickets began to sing. Helen opened her mouth just as Denny spoke.

"Sorry, go ahead," she said.

Denny smiled and inclined their head. "I was just going to say that William is a fool."

Helen's brow wrinkled. "I'm not sure I understand."

"Never mind." They stood and reached a hand out. "May I escort you home, Helen?"

She chewed her lip before nodding and accepting Denny's reach. She tucked her arm in theirs, and they began the short walk toward her house. The click of their heels filled the silence between them, and when they reached the intersection where Denny should turn toward their own house, they stopped.

"Would you like company for the rest of the way?"

Helen shook her head. "I think it's best if not. William would be unhappy knowing I ran into anyone."

Denny nodded somberly and patted the back of her hand. "I hope you find peace with him."

Helen didn't share that she had prayed to the gods for the same thing. That or an escape. She simply removed her arm from theirs and turned down her street, painfully aware of how Denny watched to make sure she made it home safely.

4

June stood behind the counter at the diner, staring at the blank wall next to the door. The white paint was chipping, revealing a drab cinder block beneath it. She looked back at the order pad in front of her. The pen in her hand had been poised to write table three's order. She quickly scribbled it down and tore the sheet from the pad. She was glad to have work, but she'd much rather be sculpting than waiting tables.

"Cheeseburger, chicken sandwich, and fry for three!" she called through the window.

Chef grunted from across the kitchen, and she went back to the register. Resting her arm on the counter and leaning down to draw on the notepad, she wrinkled her nose in disgust. No matter how many times she scrubbed the countertop, it was always sticky.

The air in the restaurant was hot, laden with the smell of burned grease and salt, and the collar of her uniform scratched her neck. She pulled at it, then reached to straighten her skirt, while her mind wandered to the gods. She wondered if Athena's battle skirt was as uncomfortable as her own, or if Artemis could move as swiftly as normal if she were to wear this godsforsaken dress. June began to doodle in the corner of the pad, sketching the outline of an ax.

June finished her little sketch and smiled at it. As she set the pen to paper to draw something else, the brass bell on the front door chimed, and she looked up to see a man walk in.

He wore a dark-blue suit with thin, white stripes and a white fedora with blue ribbon in the same almost-black shade as the rest of his attire. He took off his hat and hung it on the rack next to the door while she tore off her drawing page and straightened her skirt.

"Hey there!" June called.

The man didn't respond, instead waving his hand nonchalantly and heading to the back of the diner. He slid into an empty booth without looking back.

June sighed and shook her head. Picking up her pad and a menu from the shelf under the register, she made her way to the man's table and set the menu in front of him.

"Can I get you a drink?"

He ignored her and looked at the menu. She waited for a few seconds before tapping her foot and crossing her arms.

"I'll come back in a few minutes, then."

He nodded at the table and fiddled with a ring on his left pinky.

Turning away, June rolled her eyes and moved to the kitchen window, where Chef had just placed an order. She carefully balanced the plate of fries on her forearm before grabbing the other two plates. The women at table three smiled politely as June served them before heading back to the strange man in the suit.

Poised with her pen in hand, she put on her sweetest voice. "Are we ready to order?"

The man looked up at her and smiled, and her heart skipped a beat. He had the most striking eyes she had ever seen, in a shade of blue that could only be found in the ocean. Seafoam bordered his iris, and Aegean waves crashed around his pupil. Although he appeared young at a glance, small wrinkles creased around those breath-taking eyes. Twin streaks of silver hair met his temples, and he had the slightest indent in his chin, which accented his strong jaw-line perfectly. He looked far too handsome to be sitting in this crumbling diner.

June realized she was frozen in place and sucked a breath in before smiling back. When the man opened his mouth and spoke, a wave of dizziness came over her.

"Black coffee and a piece of pumpkin pie, please . . . Juniper?"

His coarse voice startled her, as she wasn't expecting the air of authority it commanded. She glanced down at her name tag and laughed. "Oh, yeah, I forgot I was wearing that. I actually go by June. I normally wear one that says 'June,' but I left it at home, and this was all I had in my cubby." She realized she was rambling and snapped her mouth shut.

The man's stark white teeth shone as he smiled wider. "I see. Well, it's nice to meet you, June." He dipped his head before continuing. "My name is Don."

A light blush crept into June's cheeks as she gave him a quick curtsy, pulling her skirt out on one side. "Much obliged, Don. I'll fetch your pie and coffee real quick."

"No rush, darlin'. Would you care to join me? It's getting close to dinner."

She fiddled with her pen as she glanced at the clock on the wall. She was due for a break. This might be her only chance to have one before closing.

"Yeah, I could do that."

Don nodded and turned back to the menu, and June took that as a dismissal. She quickly walked behind the counter, brain feeling fuzzy as she sliced the largest piece of pie that would be allowed and placed it gently on one of the newer dessert plates. She poured a cup of coffee—not half full like Denny insisted she do to save money, but right to the top—and made her way back to Don, careful not to spill a drop.

She ran to fetch her own mug of coffee, mixed with milk and sugar, and returned to slide into the booth opposite her new dinner partner.

The two sat together for nearly an hour, chatting about life. June learned that Don was an important businessman that lived just outside the city. He was single, his last name was Whittaker, and she assumed he made a lot of money, based on the fact he wore a nice gold bracelet that matched his ring and had a navy-blue handkerchief in his jacket pocket made of silk. He was in midtown for some business and had to get home quickly. He'd done a lot of traveling all over the world and had too many stories to share and not enough time to tell them to her. June was captivated and felt like she could tell him anything.

"So what about your parents, June? I imagine you're living with them until you find a man?" His voice sounded like sand-paper and made her smile.

"No," she replied, spinning her spoon in her mug. "My father isn't the nicest person. I hate to speak ill of him, but my mother says he was completely different before I was born. I hate how he's treated her, and frankly, he scares me. He gambles, which stresses him out, then he drinks, but breaking the law stresses him out more, so then he takes it out on my mom." June paused and looked at Don, whose eyes were trained intently on her. "My mom was—is a wonderful woman. When I was a kid, she was full of life and light. She was a gem. I think the years with my father have worn her down. She seems so . . . . empty now. I want nothing more than for her to get to be her own person again.

"When I graduated, Denny, who runs this place, offered me a job—and the apartment next door. They only had Chef working here and was tired of waiting tables. Frankly, I think they were just excited to have someone they could pay less than most. So I moved, and now I work."

Don nodded, and his half smile pulled out a dimple on his left cheek. The light brush of stubble on his jaw caught the light and made her stomach flip.

She finally decided that he had to be about forty, old enough to be her father but young enough to be as fit as his suit made him look. She was absolutely enthralled, and became even more so when he took the time to ask what she planned to do now that she was out of school.

"I think I'm going to try to get into that new art school." She propped her elbows on the table and clasped her hands under her chin, looking off dreamily. "I love sculpting, and I think I'm pretty good at it. I want to sell my pieces to collectors all over the world. My mom was an artist, although she wouldn't say it now. Her paintings made me so happy growing up, and I want to make others happy like that."

June turned her attention back to Don and noticed that he looked anxious. His knee began bouncing under the table, and he glanced at his watch.

"Hey, hun, I have to get going."

June's stomach fluttered. She wasn't sure why she felt such disappointment at that.

"Of course. I should get back to work as well." A sudden clarity hit her as Don walked away, and she looked around and realized the restaurant was empty.

Don lifted his hat from the hook and swept it on with a flourish, winking at her. "I'll be seeing you real soon, Miss Georgian."

A deep warmth crept through her cheeks as he left, and she rushed and ran behind the counter.

"Chef!" she called out.

The old man sitting in his chair by the stove raised his head from his paper.

"Where is everyone?" she asked.

He snorted and shook his head. "Served and gone. You were busy."

She felt her face flush a deeper crimson and tapped her fingers against the kitchen window. She looked around and grabbed the broom, wanting to do something helpful.

"I'm sorry, Chef. I didn't mean to get so caught up."

"S'okay. I was the same when I met my wife."

Her mind began to wander as thoughts about a future with this man crept in. Each sweep of the broom led her deeper into the daydream of a little house on the river with Don and two young boys playing in the backyard.

She let her mind drift as she began to total out the till. Chef might not spend much time in the front of the diner, but he had done an impeccable job of keeping the cash straight.

She told him as much as he hung his apron and said good night.

"I'll see you tomorrow. Dinner shift?" June asked.

Chef grunted in response, and June smiled. He was a man of few words.

She continued cashing out the till and was nearly ready to put the money in the safe when the bell jingled. She swore under her breath and stuffed the handful of cash into the mop bucket, straightening quickly; Chef should have locked the door.

Her mouth dropped into an 'o' as Don stepped into the diner and closed the door gently behind him.

"What are you doing here?" June asked.

He gave her a tight smile as he hung his hat, then stepped forward. Before he could answer, the door opened again, and two more sets of broad shoulders muscled their way in behind him. Their suits were the inverse of his—steel gray with navy pinstripes.

A flicker of frustration passed over his face, but he smoothed his hair back, and by the time he fixed his intense gaze back on June, his expression was unbothered.

"I need to talk to you, Juniper."

Her heart thudded in her chest, and she looked between the three men. "It's really just June," she said as she tried to remember the quickest route to the back door.

"Well, June," Don corrected, "I'm friends with your father. See, we have a debt to settle," he continued as he walked slowly toward the counter.

A new type of tingling started in her stomach. Not like the excited butterflies from earlier. This was a sickening, anxious tickle that made her want to throw up.

"I haven't been able to pin William down lately, and he owes me a lot of money. Do you know anything about that?" Don asked.

June shook her head and stuttered before finding her words. "No. Nothing. I'm sure I can pass along a message for you, though."

Don smiled then, wide and insincere, as he rounded the counter. "I'm sure you can, sweet thing. The money he owes me can't be collected with just a note."

June scrambled for the mop bucket and produced the handful of cash from the register. "This is all I have—well, all the diner has."

He *tsked* and shook his head, placing his large hand over her small, shaking fingers. "I don't want the diner's money. I want your daddy's." He turned briefly and nodded to the men, and they left June's vision as he walked behind her.

Before she could get out the question of where they had gone, her sentence was cut off by Don's calloused hand clamping over her mouth.

Panic rushed through her, electrocuting each nerve and limb as her mind raced, trying to remember what to do in this type of situation. His broad body pushed against her back, and the smell of strong cologne wrapped around her. Her shoulders pressed against his chest, and she realized she was having trouble breathing because his forearm was crushing her ribcage.

His voice, which had previously sounded strong and firm, was suddenly terrifying. "So here's what's gonna happen. I'll let go of you, and you're gonna lie down on that bench there." He motioned to the first booth past the end of the counter. "You're gonna lift that cute little skirt of yours and stay quiet. Got it?" A tendril of his coffee-tainted breath wrapped around to her nose, and tears welled in her eyes as he squeezed her jaw harder. She nodded as well as she could, and he chuckled. "Good."

The moment June felt the pressure release from her face, she bolted. Two steps away, she was stopped short by Don's huge hands yanking her back. He grabbed her at the waist and pulled her around, throwing her to the ground just short of a table.

He seized her hair in one hand and stuffed a handkerchief in her mouth with the other. She heard a zipper over her gasping sob and tried to scream, but the silk caught every sound, only letting air escape. As he moved and grunted, she let her mind drift off, and thought once more of the gods. Praying to Athena for strength, and Artemis for protection.

A rustling sound filled the air, the floor began to tremble, and the lights flickered, drawing June's attention up.

"What in the realms?" Don asked, tightening his grip on her waist.

A crack echoed through the air and the room was flooded with bright, white light. June was blinded, and Don was knocked away from her. He hit the floor with a thud and his heavy groans stopped.

A moment later, soft hands reached out and gripped her shaking shoulders. She flinched hard and looked up to see a woman reaching for her. She was dressed in rags and appeared worn down by time spent in the elements. June leaned forward and was pulled into her chest, too numb to care who was touching her now, as long as it wasn't *him*, and she let herself be held. Curling her hands into her chest and pulling her knees up. The woman stroked her hair and hummed, and June began to sob.

"There, there, dear. I know." Her voice was like honey mixed in warm tea.

June looked up and met the woman's hazel eyes, full of wisdom and pain. She sniffled and tried to speak, but her words were stuck in her lungs, her throat raw from crying.

"It's okay, I understand," the woman crooned. "I have you now."

June curled up again and nodded.

The woman stopped humming and whispered, "I want to give you a gift." The sky outside crackled with lightning, and thunder boomed, making June jump. Goosebumps raised on her arms again.

The woman glanced up before dropping her voice further. "Should you feel the threat of harm from any man that dares gaze into your eyes, I declare that they shall turn to stone before you." The woman leaned down and kissed June's forehead. "Just remember that revenge isn't everything, dear."

June opened her eyes. She looked up to ask what the woman meant, but she was gone in an instant. June looked around the room as if seeing it for the first time.

She had no idea what the woman meant, or how she expected her words to help, but as she stood on wobbling legs and looked at Don's silhouette splayed out on the ground, anger licked up the inside of June's stomach. She screamed, the sound echoing through the empty room, and turned, bounding out of the doorway and down the street.

She ran as fast as her legs could carry her, mind racing as the street around her blurred. Streetlights and houses flashed past her as her feet pounded the pavement. She turned left, then right, then zigzagged around a couple walking their dog, ignoring their puzzled expressions and the yelp that the terrier let out. She ran until a stitch formed in her side, slowing only when she ran straight into a woman smaller than her.

"Are you okay?" The woman's question punctured through June's eardrums and caused a dull thud to start at the base of her skull. She nodded warily before picking up a jog, limbs aching and muscles screaming in protest. She moved as fast as possible until she reached her parents' house.

June hadn't visited since she moved out, but it appeared unchanged. The white fence outside still guarded the small front yard. The mailbox still proudly held her sloppily painted flowers on it. She carefully opened the gate. Five steps took her up the walkway to the porch. Two steps took her to the door. She burst through, nearly toppling over, and looked up to meet her mother's eyes.

5

Helen stopped in the hallway, a basket of washing perched on her hip, when June pounded through the door. One look at her face and Helen knew something terrible had happened. June's green eyes were rimmed with red, and half of her thick curls were unbound and wild, while the rest were still caught in her bun. Helen dropped the basket and reached out, confused.

"Juniper?"

The girl ran to her mother, nearly knocking her off her feet, and fell into her arms.

"A man . . . he—" She choked on her words.

Helen shushed and rocked her daughter, eyes closed as she sent up a silent prayer to Apollo. With much difficulty, Helen moved her to the couch, where they curled up together. She pulled a blanket around them and rubbed her daughter's back, waiting until Juniper had calmed before whispering, "What happened?"

Juniper sniffled and looked up, pain obvious on her face. "A man, Don Whittaker, came to the diner. He—" she croaked and didn't finish her sentence.

Helen held her tight again, understanding. "Oh, honey, I'm so sorry." She could hardly finish the sentence from the pain that clogged her own throat.

Juniper shook her head but seemed unable to speak, and her back was tensed, as if she was going to leap away and run. It was a long minute before she sniffed and whispered, "He told me it was a message to Dad."

Helen stiffened at the knowledge that this harm was done in the name of the man who was supposed to protect Juniper most. She realized that she had stopped rubbing circles on June's back, so she resumed the motion again, trying to remember if William had ever said anything about a man named Don.

But William never spoke about his activities outside of the home. Anger rose, and her cheeks flushed.

She had excused all of William's bad features, choosing to shoulder the burden and shield Juniper from him, but now . . . he would risk their safety for his own selfish reasons? What was wrong with him! How could he do this? Allowing harm to come to their daughter was as bad as hurting her himself. When William got home, she would make him answer for his crimes.

The moment came sooner than expected. Just as Helen opened her mouth to reassure June that she was safe now, she heard the front door open. Her entire body went still, heat flushed through her, and she flicked her eyes to the clock above the entryway. Dinner should have been ready a long time ago. This was the first evening in ten years that the smell of a warm meal wasn't wafting through the house upon William's arrival. He seemed to notice too, as he stopped in the middle of removing his shoes and looked at the scene in front of him, apparently confused.

Helen didn't move from her position as her eyes trained on her husband. Her feet were pulled up on the couch, with June lying in her lap.

They locked eyes, and Helen flinched as anger took over his features. He lifted his shoe in the air and shook it at his wife. "What do you think you're doing?"

She began to answer but snapped her mouth closed to duck her head as the shoe flew toward her. It hit the wall behind the couch with a dull thud. William balled his fists and moved toward Helen quickly. She managed to yell, "Will, stop!" before his hand closed around her arm.

He dragged her upward, pulling her face an inch away from his, and repeated through gritted teeth, "What do you think you're doing?"

June slumped on the couch, and Helen did her best to shield her daughter from William's view.

Helen, fully pulled out of her ten-year reverie, spat back, "Helping our daughter."

William threw Helen backward, causing her to fall to the ground. She caught herself and stood quickly, ready to challenge her husband. The smell of bourbon wafted from him, and she shook her head. "You're drunk. Go to bed."

William stepped forward and slapped her across the face. "You do not speak to me that way, woman." He stepped past her and eyed June, who was still lying on the couch.

He scoffed and stalked into the kitchen, Helen trailing behind him. She planted her feet in the doorway as he looked at the empty stove. "Who the hell is Don Whittaker, and what was he doing at the diner?"

William whirled around, his expression unreadable. "How do you know that name?"

"Tell me, William, how much money was worth putting our family in harm's way? How big of a prize made our inevitable pain worth it to you?" She threw her words at him before turning to go back to June.

William's hand closed around her arm like a vise just a step out of the kitchen, and he yanked her to the hallway and threw her to the ground. Before she could react, he kicked her hard in the stomach, spit foaming at his lips as he screeched, "How dare you welcome me home"—he kicked again—"with only an accusation." He kicked Helen a third time, and the veil that had previously lifted dropped back over her, forcing her senses to numb themselves to the feeling of his foot connecting with her ribs.

She barely registered the bursts of pain as William leaned down and picked her up by the hair, dragging her back to the living room. She could only mumble a protest as June stood from the couch and yelled, "Stop!"

William froze in place, eyes locked with his daughter's. She had never said a word during these aggressions with Helen before. Helen raised her hand and tried to croak out, "No!" but William stopped only long enough to let go of her and swing his arm around, hand balled in a fist, toward June.

William's fist never made contact.

He stilled, his torso moving so slowly before stuttering to a stop. He glanced down, and a panicked expression replaced his angry one. Helen followed his gaze and sucked in a sharp breath, and she heard a similar gasp from June.

His foot appeared to be solid stone, and the gray rock was quickly moving upward. His slacks looked as if someone had dipped them in concrete. His fear-filled eyes flicked between the women, and he unballed his fist to reach out.

Helen watched in disbelief and mute horror as gray veins replaced blue, blond hair turned white, and the sneer on William's face stayed there, frozen in time. William looked like a work of art—a terrifying piece, but art nonetheless. She quickly scrambled up and ran to June, hugging the girl tightly as they both stared at the statue that was William Georgian.

They stood together like that for a long while. Helen said nothing about the prayers she had sent to the gods for years to get her out of her marriage, but her mind still raced. How did this happen? Was it divine intervention? Had June done something?

No, that wouldn't be possible.

It wasn't until the clock on the wall chimed loudly that she finally moved. She pulled away and looked at her daughter. June gave her hand a squeeze, and Helen offered her a small smile, trying to gather her senses.

"Dinner?" she asked.

June nodded.

6

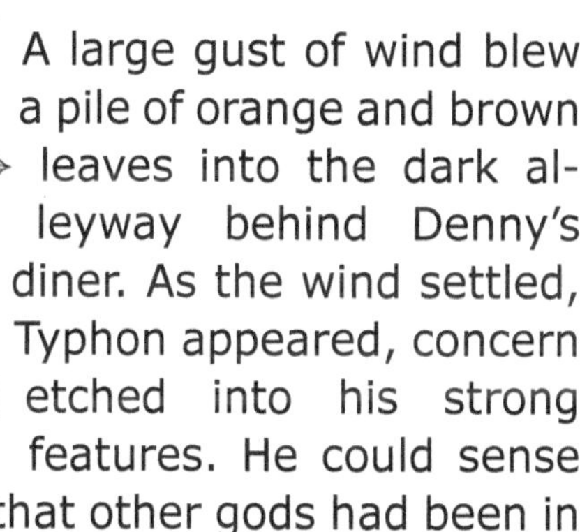

A large gust of wind blew a pile of orange and brown leaves into the dark alleyway behind Denny's diner. As the wind settled, Typhon appeared, concern etched into his strong features. He could sense that other gods had been in the area tonight, along with June, and his mind jumped to the worst conclusion.

He strode toward the diner when a shadow emerged from his left. Whirling quickly, he saw a drab-looking woman step toward him. Her eyes, which were the only bright thing about her, twinkled at him in the low light.

Typhon inclined his head and smiled. "Hello, Athena."

The woman straightened, letting the disguise of dirty cloth fall off to reveal a tall, strong body clad in a leather skirt and chest plate. "Typhon. Tsk tsk."

Typhon's face fell as she crossed her arms. "What happened?"

"Where were you?"

Typhon looked around helplessly. "There was a storm to attend to. Where's Juniper? Is she okay?" He looked at Athena, and her face softened. She reached out a hand and patted his shoulder. He could only feel that something had happened to June while he was away, but not the extent of damage.

"I couldn't make it before he hurt her. But I gave her something to help."

Panic took over the god's features as he tried to think of what on Olympus Athena could have done.

"It's okay, Ty. She'll be fine. But next time . . . well, don't let next time happen. I may not be the one to come and take care of her." She gave him a knowing look and turned.

"Wait, what happened?"

She looked at him again. This time, her features told a story of pain and desperation. She took one step forward, into a shaft of moonlight, and moved as if to shift away. Before she could, thunder boomed around them. Athena looked at Typhon, startled, and lightning flared across the sky. His eyes widened at the clear call from Zeus.

"What did you do?" he pressed.

She opened her mouth as a cloud moved in front of the moon. In the next moment, she was gone with the light, leaving Typhon alone.

His brow twitched and as he stepped down the alley to find June, he felt the pull of a summoning from Zeus, and was swept up in a gust of wind.

He landed hard next to Athena, throwing his hand to shield his eyes from the bright sun of Olympus, which was blinding in contrast to the night he had just been in.

"You!" Zeus' voice boomed around him.

Typhon's heart sank, and his eyes snapped around the room. He'd landed in the Great Hall of Olympus, in front of the Olympic Council's seats. The ruling twelve, or what was left of them, anyway, sat around him and Athena. Each god was taller and more commanding than the last, in their various godly forms with blue skin here and flashing eyes there.

"Athena, my child, what have you done?" Zeus' eyes softened before he stood from his chair, which sat on a raised dais. "You gifted a mortal with the power of the gods?"

Though phrased as a question, his voice held a demand, and his face was etched with concern as he stepped down from his pedestal. Typhon had to look up as the larger god began to shrink from his Olympian form. The purple hue in his skin faded, and the lightning bolts arcing across his skin tucked back into his veins.

"She was being attacked—"

Zeus raised a hand to quiet Athena's defense and turned to Typhon.

"And you. I let your blessing for the human slip before, on the oath that you would prevent situations like this. We are not meant to meddle directly in mortal affairs. Yet you abandoned your charge and another god took your place. Two blessings to one mortal? Unacceptable."

"Yes, but—"

Again, Zeus interrupted. "Athena will face trial for her crimes against Olympus."

Athena's and Typhon's jaws dropped open simultaneously.

"As you are respected elders of this realm, I won't go as far as sending you to Underworld to wait, but I do not want you leaving Olympus." He turned to Typhon. "For your part, there will be no more gifts, blessings, or interference with the mortals. If it would require divine intervention, don't do it. Or you will also find yourself on trial. Understood?"

"Yes," Typhon and Athena spoke together.

Zeus stomped away and Typhon glanced at his niece, a pained expression twisting his features. "You should have stayed out of it," he chastised.

Athena threw her hands up, taking off toward her home. "I should have let him kill her? Right," she mumbled under her breath.

Typhon ran to keep on her heels, shaking his head. "No, I just—I'm frustrated."

He sighed heavily and stopped in front of her. "I don't know what I'll do if Zeus bans me from Olympus, but I owe Juniper and Helen."

"You've created your own mess," she scoffed. "Why do you have such an attachment, anyway?"

Typhon ran a hand through his hair, flattening the pieces that stuck up, and cleared his throat. "William wouldn't be so much trouble if it weren't for me. I can't keep digging their hole any deeper."

"Your storms have caused far worse damage than an angry father," Athena said. "You simply looked too close at the Georgians."

He nodded, but pursed his lips. He knew it had to be deeper than that. Athena gazed into his eyes for a moment longer before turning and leaving him in the middle of the Great Hall.

7

June carefully spooned bites of leftover stew into her mouth. The tender meat and spiced broth fell to sawdust on her tongue, and she had to force herself through the motions of eating.

They ate in silence, each taking turns to cast a glance at William. Helen had drawn the curtains shut, making sure no one could see the statue in the middle of the living room.

Helen broke the silence first, pulling June's attention. "Do you think it can be undone?" Her voice sounded anxious, and June wasn't sure if it was because Helen wanted William back or because she didn't.

She shrugged. "I'm not sure. I wouldn't think so."

Helen nodded solemnly and returned her attention to her bowl. Suddenly she dropped her spoon, a look of horror on her face. "What do we do with him?"

June forced a small smile that felt more like a grimace and reached across the table to squeeze her mother's hand. "I'll figure it out, don't worry."

Helen frowned, but she resumed eating.

The two women stood in front of William and looked at him, sizing up how to move him. His face was eerie—frozen in the expression of rage and fear he'd worn when he had turned on June. One hand still hung down, while the other was outstretched. Dark veins ran through the marble, and where the light shone on it, the marble was stark white. June finally shuddered and suggested wrapping him in blankets before anything. Helen agreed and ran to the hall closet.

They worked together to wrap him up, and when an old comforter was secured around his shoulders, Helen cleared her throat. "You know, he wasn't always a bad man. Once upon a time, he was truly amazing. He helped so much to prepare for your birth. I'm not sure what happened to him today—if you did something or a god decided to intervene—but I'm going to refrain from asking questions. I don't want to be involved unless you're in trouble and need help." She paused, then looked at June sadly. "I just want you to know that he wasn't always bad."

June nodded slightly. "Thanks, Mom." But she couldn't help the anger that crept in at the thought that, even now, her mother was still making excuses for him.

"I know it was hard to grow up with him," Helen whispered, securing a pillowcase over William's head, "and I'm sorry I never had the strength to leave."

June reached out and caught her mother's hand, eyes hard as she looked her in the eye. "Don't ever apologize. You did your best, I know that. And quite frankly, I'm glad he's gone." Suddenly a twisted giggle burst from June's chest, driven out by exhaustion and disbelief. "I'm GLAD he's gone!" she exclaimed.

Helen's face contorted strangely before she began to laugh as well. They both hunched over, an arm on each other's shoulder, laughing as the heavy air that had filled the house for years lifted. June felt lighter, and she knew Helen must too.

Helen recovered first, taking a shaky breath and pulling June in for a hug. "Thank you," she whispered into June's half-loose pile of curls. "I don't know how you managed to free us from him, but thank you."

June said nothing. She breathed in the scent of her mother—warm vanilla and fresh bread, now mixed with salt from tears—and nestled in, enjoying the embrace. She didn't know what she had done either, but she was grateful that at least it had done her mother some good. She finally pulled back and motioned at William. "We should probably move him."

Helen's brow furrowed, and she opened her mouth to speak, but June cut her off. "It's okay, Mom. I can handle it."

Helen's mouth set in a frown, and she reached out to grasp both of June's shoulders. "Juniper Georgian, I have no doubt in my mind that you can handle anything thrown at you. But I'm worried. You shouldn't have to deal with what may come from this."

June smiled and mimicked Helen, placing her hands on her mother's shoulders. "Mother, it's okay."

Helen held her gaze for a long moment before sighing. "Okay. But you better take his truck." She laughed uneasily, some of the tension in her shoulders dissipating as she led the way to the garage. "I can comfortably say that neither your father nor I imagined it would be used for this when we went to pick it up."

June let out a low whistle when the side door swung open to reveal the brand-new '26 Model TT. She rubbed the back of her neck and looked over the shiny green paint and fresh tires. William had said that since he worked at a manufacturing plant, he had gotten a good deal. She wondered if it was actually related to gambling, but she refrained from asking and risking the upset it might bring Helen.

She was exhausted, and with good reason. William weighed at least two hundred pounds, and it was well into the early hours of the morning when they began dragging him through the house. But they still had to load him into the truck bed, so the two women moved to either side of his stone form. Helen reached up and pulled his head down, leaning his feet at an angle so June could get her hands under to lift.

Helen grunted. "Ready?"

June heaved her half of the stone up, and the air in her lungs whooshed out as she shuffled to the truck bed, trying to keep her back straight. She was glad he wasn't as heavy as proper marble, but, gods, it was hard to carry an entire human-sized statue. She tried to set the foot end of him down gently, but a muffled clunk echoed out. She moved quickly to Helen's side and helped shove William into the bed.

When they pushed him in as far as possible, his head still hung over the edge of the tailgate. They stopped and looked at him. Good gods, if someone had told her that one day she'd be moving her father's corpse in the middle of the night, she would have slapped them.

Helen wrapped an arm around June and pulled her from her thoughts. "Will you be okay? Would you like me to come with you?"

She shook her head. "No, I'll be fine. Don't worry. But—" She pulled back and looked Helen in the eye. "It may be best not to tell anyone. I don't know what exactly happened, but I don't want to risk the wrong person finding out."

Helen nodded and gave June one last squeeze before letting go. "Be safe," she whispered.

June smiled and jumped into the truck, setting it in gear and rolling backward from the driveway. She gave a small wave to Helen before sputtering down the road.

The drive only took a few minutes in the nearly new truck. It still amazed June just how fast they could travel now. The last car they had was from before she was born, and it was as slow as a snail compared to this.

June pulled up in front of the diner, parking parallel to the front door so it would be easier to pull William in. Once stopped, she gripped the wheel tightly with both hands, leaning her forehead against it. What was she to do? The woman in the diner had clearly been serious about her blessing. She thought back to how it had felt, like some divine power was around her, and wondered if the woman in rags had actually been a goddess. She sighed and lifted her head from the wheel, turning to look in the restaurant. It was closed, and she knew Denny wouldn't be here for hours to open.

June finally let go of the steering wheel and turned to clamber down from the truck. As she reached for the handle and lifted her eyes, they met a pair of stormy ones. She let out a shriek and threw her hand to her heart. She popped the handle of the door and jumped out, nearly toppling Ty.

"You scared the living daylights out of me!"

"Sorry, kiddo." He looked around, and his brow furrowed. "What's going on here?"

June ran her hand up her neck, cocking her head and grimacing. "Um, I'm not really sure how to explain that." She pushed past

Ty and stopped by the bed of the truck. "This is going to sound insane, and you'll probably think I'm crazy. Honestly, I'm amazed Mom didn't—"

Ty silenced her with a hand on her shoulder. "You would be amazed at what I find insane and what I don't."

June took a deep breath and nodded. She flourished her arm over William's statue. "Meet my new, and some may say improved, father." A nervous laugh forced its way through her chest, and she tried to cover it with a cough.

Ty raised an eyebrow and pulled back the pillowcase covering William's head. As soon as he saw what lay under the cloth, his eyes widened, and he swore, wiping a hand down his red beard.

"What have you done?" he said so softly that she wondered if he was even speaking to her.

June chewed her bottom lip and watched Ty pace for a moment before moving to drag William from the truck bed.

"What are you doing!" Ty exclaimed as she yanked William a foot toward her.

She heaved a breath and bit out, "Moving him."

Another hard yank on his neck, and he was tottering precariously on the edge of the truck bed. His top half leaned down toward the ground, and she leaped back, nearly knocking Ty over.

"Shit!" she yelled. She bit the inside of her cheek as time slowed and William fell.

The solid stone statue crashed down against the slick pavement, knocking off his outstretched arm. June threw her hands up to cover her mouth as the hand bounced once before shattering into a thousand tiny shards, sending an echo slicing through the cool air. June stood rooted in place, staring in horror at her father's broken arm.

Ty stepped up and cleared his throat, placing a hand on her lower back and causing her to jump. "Maybe I should help."

June shot a dirty look at his back as he stepped forward and bent down, gripping William by the middle and pulling him up.

"You couldn't offer to help before I broke my dad?"

Ty grunted in response, and June's jaw dropped as she watched him pull the marble out of the bed and set it carefully on the road behind the truck. He turned around, and she noticed his brow was clear of sweat.

He muttered under his breath. "Athena . . ."

June snapped her head up. "What? What did you say?"

Ty turned and looked at her, appearing to struggle for words. He released a loud breath. "Nothing. Let's get William moved."

June moved to block his path and planted her hands on her hips. "No, you said 'Athena.' Why?"

Typhon looked uncomfortable, and he moved to step around her, but she mirrored his steps and raised her chin defiantly, looking her oldest friend directly in the eye.

"Ty, so help me. I have had an awful day, and if you don't tell me what you're talking about, I'll figure out how this thing works and you can join my dad."

Typhon's eyebrows shot up, and she bit her lip, wondering if she'd gone too far.

"Okay, fine." He heaved a sigh, yanking William toward the diner. "Let's go take a seat," he said.

8

"I need you to keep an open mind."

June nodded, sliding into the booth across from Typhon.

"I am going to sound crazy."

"You didn't think I was crazy." June's eyes softened, and Typhon's heart raced.

He was about to share forbidden information with her. Well, he thought it was forbidden. He took a deep breath in. She deserved to know what she'd been thrown into. If Zeus would call informing her interfering, then he would just have to stand trial.

"There is more to this world than what you see."

June rolled her eyes, but he ignored it, cleared his throat, and continued.

"You are an extremely smart girl, I wouldn't be surprised if you already knew, but my name is actually Typhon. I am the Titan God—"

"Of Wind and Storm?" June finished for him. "We learned about you in school. I've wondered for years if you were him."

Typhon smiled. Good old public education. "Well, there's more. But . . . I didn't know about this." He motioned at William before reaching across the table to hold June's hand. "I'm so sorry I wasn't around to stop it."

June patted his hand in answer, face as stonelike as her father's. She wasn't ready to think of what Don had done.

"I saw Athena after whatever she did to you, but she didn't tell me what happened, only that she came to help."

At that, June's jaw dropped, and she sprang up. "I knew it! I prayed to her, and I knew that woman was a god!"

Typhon grimaced. Were they all really that obvious? "Athena stepped in since I wasn't there, and while I don't agree with her methods, I am glad she could comfort you at the very least. Normally, gods don't get in the way of mortal affairs, or even hang around a mortal life. But I knew you would be special the day you were born. Your father did something so wild, so fantastical, that I knew his child would be both interesting and destined for great things."

June screwed up her face at that. "What do you mean?"

Typhon leaned forward, dropping his voice for emphasis. "He saw me . . . in my natural form."

June looked as though she ate something sour. "Do you mean naked?" she whispered, sounding horrified.

Typhon leaned back and let out a roar of laughter, his chest heaving and the sound bouncing off the walls around as a small puff of wind swirled around them. He laughed while June's face flushed. He coughed, shaking his head. When he finally calmed enough to take a deep breath, the swirl of air disappeared. "No, June. Even better. He saw me in my godly form. Not tethered to a human body."

June's jaw dropped yet again. "What do you mean? Like, just in the sky?"

Typhon nodded. "Something like that. More like, made of air. The thing is, normally when mortals gaze upon a god that way, they go mad. They just . . . immediately lose their minds. The last one actually went on a killing spree."

June leaned back, and Typhon watched a nerve twitch in her jaw. He furrowed his brow, worried. What if she didn't take this as well as it seemed a moment ago? Too late now.

"Do you think that's why Dad went so . . . bad?" She swallowed hard and looked at him, and his heart twinged again.

"I don't know." He watched as she picked at her thumbnail, her eyes glazing over. He didn't want it to be the case. William had seemed so sturdy the night his storm raged on Leonard Street.

Typhon was trying to save the family from a stray tree that nearly flattened their house. The only reason William had the opportunity to see Typhon on the wind was because he had been in the living room while Helen gave birth in a different room.

He cleared his throat, and she snapped her attention back to him as he went on. "Either way, I'm afraid that you are now caught in the middle of something terrible. See, none of us had blessed a mortal in centuries. You were the first."

June's brows furrowed.

"When you were born, I blessed you with protection," he said in response to the confusion on her face. "I had to check that your father was okay after seeing me, and there you were. Now, not only have I been involved, but so has Athena, and I wouldn't be surprised if some others step in to play. They, uh—" He hesitated, embarrassed on behalf of his kind. "They're a nosy bunch and like to get involved."

June stared at him with a blank expression.

Typhon sighed. "I worry that there is something sinister at play."

"What do you mean?" June asked.

"A long time ago, the central three ruled Olympus side by side." Typhon paused and waited for a heartbeat, but June said nothing.

"Zeus, Poseidon, and Hades. I'm sure you're quite familiar with Hades' story—sent to rule over Underworld, so on and so forth." June nodded. "Well, Poseidon was exiled as well. He tried to start an uprising against Zeus, wanting to rule more than just the seas. See, while Hades got souls and Zeus got mortals and Olympus, Poseidon was shuffled to the side, told to stick to water and fish, and, eventually, he grew bored."

"What does this have to do with me?"

Typhon raised a finger and continued. "He sent some of his followers down into Underworld to steal from Hades. They took creatures of all sorts from him—terrifying beasts that had previously died and become experiments for new torturers. He stole from the other gods as well, taking prophecy from one of Apollo's oracles, wisdom and foresight from Athena, and recruiting some of Artemis' warriors."

June's eyes widened at this, but she kept quiet.

"Zeus found out, but only right before Poseidon raised an army against him. Much of Olympus fell, and good people died. We lost gods, Olympians, and titans, but inevitably, Poseidon lost. He was forced from the divine city and cast down to Earth. Some other gods followed—choosing to try the mortal, or semi-mortal life, since it was something new and exciting. Others went out of allegiance to him, but Poseidon was tied to a mortal body. Unlike the rest of us that may come and go as we please, he is stuck here, living many lives over and over again, his essence continuing from body to body until someone breaks the cycle.

"He's gotten worse over the years. He's grown powerful here on Earth. Now he heads the mob."

June raised her hands, forcing him to pause. "You mean to tell me that a god is responsible for all the bad crap that happens here?"

Typhon shrugged. "Sort of. He's not tied to everything, per se, just . . . a lot. Since he maintains his soul, his essence, through all his lives, he holds the same memories, motivations, and ideals as before. But it's all gotten terribly worse. We've all watched him over time and believe he intends to fully conquer Earth as his own. To turn it into his own Olympus. While he really only holds this city right now, and some farther south, he has set up such an intricate network throughout the country that he could very well take it as his. There's more to go into with this later on, but for now, here's the problem: all of us sort of have a marker that alerts other gods where we've been. I'm not sure of *exactly* what happened here tonight, but I was shocked when I did some looking around, because along with mine and Athena's marks were Poseidon's." Typhon paused and looked at June, who had a mixture of confusion and anger playing across her face.

"Don . . ."

Typhon nodded.

"You mean to tell me that *the* god, one of the top three, Poseidon, came here to . . . to—" Her words fell off, and fury etched its way onto her face.

Typhon's throat bobbed. He didn't want to ask details, given her reaction, but he knew it couldn't have been anything good. "I'm not sure why. His involvement is so deeply entrenched here that it could be for any number . . ." He trailed off as June rose suddenly, turning to pace about the restaurant.

"A god would do that?" She threw her arms in the air as Typhon nodded.

"The big ones can get away with whatever they want."

She dropped her arms and looked at the floor, muttering something that he didn't hear, before striding behind the service counter. Ty cocked his head to look and was shocked to see her emerge with a baseball bat—the same one he had given her as defense in case of emergency during work.

June strode to William and propped the bat on her shoulder. Her body shook, and she loosed a loud scream that echoed off the diner walls before dropping the bat down and swinging it wide.

It flew into William's ribcage with a loud shattering sound, and bits of his now stone shirt flew off, crumbling to the ground in a shower of dust.

"June—" Typhon half stood, to try and bring her back.

He was cut off by another blow, this time to the side of William's face. His entire cheek and part of his eye socket fell, some of it getting stuck on his shoulder.

She dropped the bat and let the head rest on the floor as she screamed again. Typhon could hear the agony in her voice, and his heart thumped loudly. The power of her yell reverberated through the air and made his bones ache. He wanted to reach out, and stepped forward to do so, but she picked the bat up again, this time spinning to point it at Typhon. She let out a mirthless laugh, sounding deranged as she yelled, "If the gods want to play games, Typhon, then I'll play games!"

She spun quickly, taking the bat with her, and slammed it into William's leg, taking his calf out completely with one blow. Marble dust flew around her, coating her dark hair and already dirty skirt, and making gray mud in the tear tracks down her face.

"June-bee?"

June didn't respond.

"Please, stop."

His plea fell to the floor between them as she moved to swing the bat again. He stepped forward once more and hesitated. Maybe space would be best. He had never seen her so angry. He could feel the air pushing against her in an effort to slow her down, and his tongue was heavy from the thought of trying to step in. He moved to the door as she raised the bat above her head and slammed it down on the tile floor, shrieking again.

The bell on the handle sounded as Typhon brushed it with an air current, and she still didn't look. Typhon sighed and spun up in a puff, lapping around the diner once before whizzing under the door.

June screamed again, and Typhon carried the sound on his breeze as he floated down the street.

9

The muscles in June's arms screamed for rest, and she obliged and stopped swinging the bat, releasing a breath and shoving her sweat-matted hair from her forehead. Dust filled the air around her, pluming from the floor where she stepped back. She bent over and stretched her back, realizing just how much she ached, and took in the broken pieces of stone scattered around her feet.

When she stood straight again, she sucked in a breath as she met the shocked expression on her father's face. Contorted somewhere between rage and fear, his skin was etched with fine wrinkles—stark white and unmoving. The thin veins that reached from his hairline toward his brows when he yelled had turned from blue to dark gray, and even his clothing was as solid as any rock that June could pick up from outside.

She blew out another breath of air and looked to the ceiling, to the skies beyond, and wondered if Athena could see her.

"Is this what you intended? I never wanted to become a murderer," June yelled.

The air was still around her for a moment before she began to shuffle around. She swiped a finger across William's shoulder, and her heart rate ticked up at the sight of gathered marble dust on her fingertip. She squinted at the crevices in his shirt filled with the fine powder before backing away and heading for the utility closet in the kitchen.

Cleaning up from her fit of emotion was nearly as taxing on her body as the rage itself. Marble dust settled into every nook and cranny of the diner, including the crevices of the upholstered seats and behind the register. June found herself sweeping multiple times, between wiping dust off the surfaces with a damp rag.

She stopped once to sit back on her ankles and look around. The moon was beginning to set, and Apollo was likely preparing to raise the sun over the horizon, lending only a sliver of light through the diner window that faced the street. Denny would be in shortly to open the diner to the early morning customers. Despite her effort to scrub the evidence away that she'd nearly destroyed a statue in the dining room, she could still see dust settling down from the air as she held her breath.

She cursed, sending a plume up from the table in front of her face, before turning back to the chair she'd been scrubbing at.

As she plunged her rag back into the bucket and watched white powder expunge itself from the cloth, tinting the water a more opaque shade of gray, tears pricked her eyes.

June was slowly wiping up remnants of her father and throwing him down the drain. With every swipe of her cloth, she was mixing him with tap water before washing him into the city's sewer line. She glanced over at the broken pieces of his body that she'd gathered and tried to make out his features through her blurred vision.

William hadn't been a kind man, but did he deserve this fate?

She jumped as metal grated in the door and threw her rag down, standing as the bell rang and Denny stepped into the diner.

They stopped two steps in, letting the door clang behind them as they took in the scene.

"What happened here?" they asked.

"Would you believe that the diner was broken into and I was attacked?" June returned.

Denny approached slowly, setting their keys down, and motioning to the stone form of her father. "And this?"

"An art project gone wrong?"

They looked around once more, and the raw ache crept up the back of June's throat again. She bit her lip as stinging droplets began to cut their way through the dust coating her cheeks, and Denny's eyes fell to her.

"Go home, I'll finish cleaning up," they said with a quiet voice.

She nodded once, moving to walk past before they grabbed her arm.

"Juniper—I'm not sure what happened here, but you can trust me." She flinched back and quickly smoothed her hands over her skirt to cover the motion.

"Thanks, Denny."

June slept fitfully for hours, from the time there were pink hues in the sky through its period of stark blueness, until purple started to tinge the horizon.

She woke slowly, bleary-eyed with stars hazing her vision, and more exhausted than when she went to sleep. Her muscles groaned in protest as she rose from the bed. She took two steps before she had to lean down to examine herself. Heavy purple bruises were blooming on her knees, and bruises lined her hips and the back of her neck where Don had held her. She looked at her face in her corner mirror and frowned. Dark bags under her eyes begged for more rest. Her lips were cracked from chapping, and her eyes were as bloodshot as an alcoholic's. Her mind flashed back to the times she'd walked in to see her mother examining her own bruises in a mirror, and she grimaced. Helen's skin was a bit darker than hers, and marks only really showed for a day before blending in. For a moment, June wished she was the same.

She shook the memory from her mind and pulled a modest dress on. As she pulled the sleeves down as far as possible to cover the bruises on her wrists, she remembered Helen pulling at her own sleeves in almost the same manner.

She swallowed and turned away from herself. The late evening light caught her eye and she rushed through her apartment quickly, taking the stairs down to street level two at a time, before walking next door to the diner. She was far overdue for work.

As June approached the front door, her feet stopped moving, and she found herself frozen in a way she'd never experienced. As her hand hovered over the door handle, she felt the imprint of Don's hands on her again, curled in the same manner as her fingers were on the cool brass under them.

She willed herself to move as blood rushed through her ears and her heart beat loudly through the back of her skull. One, two, five beats she counted before she felt like she could take a deep breath and press the handle down, and the bell's jingle released her from the remainder of the spell.

June was grateful to find the main dining room empty, and a peek into the adjoining room revealed just one guest sitting alone in a booth.

"Juniper." Denny's voice was smooth, as always, but held a warning.

Her eyes snapped to where they stood behind the register, before sliding to her father's form just to the left. She shuddered and sulked forward.

"I'm sorry—"

"How are you feeling?" Their question cut her off, and she blanched, caught off guard.

"Better, I think. I was going to apologize."

Denny waved their hand. "It could have been worse, but I would like an explanation. When you're ready, of course."

Juniper dipped her head and opened her mouth to speak, searching for the words when the door opened.

Denny jutted their chin out, a small smile playing up on their smooth face. "You have a visitor."

June's heart rate increased, and fear dripped cold through her veins as she turned, but relief flooded through her upon seeing the warm brown eyes of her mother shielded by a floppy hat.

She strode over and looped their arms together before leading Helen to a table. "What are you doing here?"

"I wanted to check in. I didn't hear from you today, and I was worried," Helen whispered.

June nodded and looked at Denny as she stood awkwardly in front of the seat where Helen had sat down. Denny waved his hand, and she sat.

June looked at her hands as she spoke. "I'm sore, and bone-tired. I don't know, it was a lot."

Helen reached a hand across the table and nodded. "I can't ever say enough how sorry I am that you're involved in our troubles."

"We are in this together," June reassured her.

Helen wrapped their hands together and smiled warmly up at Denny as they placed two cups of coffee in front of them—just over half full.

Helen lifted one with a shaking hand, almost splashing up to the edge as she sipped.

"I need to confess something," she said, still in a low voice.

June cocked her head and leaned in.

"I feel it makes me a bad person. I'm relieved that he is gone." Helen's shoulders sagged as she looked at the table, and a beat passed between them.

"I'm glad you have an escape now, without having to leave on your own, Mom," June said. Although the pain from the attack had cut her deeply, and she didn't know that she would ever fully recover, she was glad that her father wouldn't hurt Helen anymore. "What will you do? I know we need to work out the extent of the consequences, but otherwise?"

Helen's eyes brightened, and she lifted a shoulder. "I suppose . . . live."

10

Typhon drifted above the skylight window to his home as he looked over the sprawling green hills of Olympus, contemplating. Was Athena about to be stripped of her power? Or was he? He hadn't really done anything, but maybe that was the problem. Zeus had ordered he not interfere anymore . . . Then again, he felt Zeus had been looking for a reason to rid Olympus of him like his brothers since the Titan's War. But Athena was Zeus' creation, his daughter, and he loved her.

He looped on the breeze over the gold-capped roof of the city, ducking to fly beside the outer wall as a group of Nephelai shot by above, before he made his way toward the Great Hall once more. He'd seriously considered not attending Athena's trial. A small part of him thought that it would serve her right for putting herself in between him and his charge. But in his deepest heart, he knew that judgment was wrong. As much as Athena enjoyed creating heroes, he couldn't make himself believe she was trying to do so for June. At the end of the day, Athena may have saved June.

The hall was buzzing when he finally landed, and he sucked in a sharp breath, growing slightly into his Olympian form to combat the overcrowding that blocked his view.

A bench had been erected between where he stood and Zeus' pedestal, and chained to the bench by her ankles sat Athena.

Typhon's gaze traveled quickly over the room—Athena's head hung, and her long hair draped around her face, blocking her eyes from view. Though every piece of furniture in the room was made from the same gold-swirled marble as the floors themselves, the chains around her legs were black, lending a harsh undertone to the scene. Were the chains from Hephaestus' shop? Or were they simply brought from the mortal realm for show?

"Silence!" Zeus' voice boomed out over the crowd, and the chatter that filled the room died.

"Olympus and the mortal realm have existed peacefully thus far. They offer us their loyalty, worship, and most importantly, do not infringe on our boundaries, as they are unaware of the true nature of our existence. Conversely, there is a limit in how much we impede on the mortal realm. The limit to which we exist there must be maintained, as well as the depth of our relationships."

Zeus' gaze fell to Typhon then.

"I—We, as your Council—work very hard to protect this delicate balance. But it is vital that you uphold your part as Olympians. And as Olympians you have been granted abilities that those mortals might deem otherworldly, even supernatural. The modern era that their realm has entered into is not as it once was. We cannot share our strengths as we once could, without repercussions. We cannot have relations as we once could. Athena has just learned this lesson, and the Fates have begun to weave new strings from her mistake."

A collective gasp filled the high, empty ceiling.

"We have gathered to charge Athena with her crimes against Olympus." Zeus focused his attention on Athena, lowering his voice just slightly. "Athena, before the Council hears your case, do you have anything to say?"

The silence that followed his question was deafening as the crowd held their breath. Typhon scanned over the heads in the room, looking for any sign of outburst, but everyone was waiting as anxiously as him.

"I stand by what I did. I saved her from a worser fate at the hands of Poseidon, and stepped in as he attacked her." Athena spoke softly, but her words still carried to the back of the room.

Sharp breaths sounded off a moment before the uproar began. Bodies thrashed around him, and expletives were thrown toward the Council—some directed at Athena, some at Zeus. Typhon was rooted in place as the meaning of her words sunk in. He was sure the crowd didn't know who they were meant to be angry with; they'd just heard the name of their greatest traitor and wanted to riot.

"SILENCE!" Zeus' yell reverberated through the hall and shook the floor, sending the Olympians around Typhon careening into one another as they shushed each other.

"We are here for a trial and will hear all details before the Council comes to a conclusion. Any spectators that interrupt or impede the proceedings will be forced to leave."

He turned to the other seats surrounding the dais where Athena sat—though many were empty—and addressed Apollo. "Please read the charges."

Apollo hesitated for a moment before he unfurled a roll of paper. "Olympus charges Athena with excessive interference in the affairs of mortals, overextension of fulfilling or offering blessings to a mortal, infringing on another god's blessing and/or agreement with a mortal or equal being, and finally, defying the agreement with Olympus written in a previous trial for similar matters." Apollo swallowed hard and looked at Athena, who finally raised her head.

Typhon swore under his breath and began to weave through the crowd. He'd forgotten that she'd already stood trial before. Why hadn't Zeus called him as a witness to testify on Athena's behalf, or why hadn't she? He was as involved in this as she was; it was his mortal that had been affected.

As he reached the middle of the crowd, he realized that Zeus had begun speaking again. "—Not your first offense?"

Typhon froze to watch Athena shake her head.

"I have helped other mortals," she confirmed.

"I'm going to call on a witness to the damage you've done. First, you have the opportunity to recount your own version of events," Zeus said.

Typhon released a breath of relief. He was the only witness, so hopefully his testimony would aid her in getting out of the situation.

"There was a mortal in danger," Athena started, looking around the room. Not a muscle moved among the crowd as she spoke. "I was performing my duty, as a god, and acting on a prayer. Though not a direct act of war, the attack performed was a result of and possibly in anticipation of.

Poseidon may be bound to a mortal body, but he is not one. We must remember that this was a god attacking a lesser being. A being that asked for protection."

The crowd seized around Typhon at the mention of the previous God of the Sea's name, and he looked toward a particularly uncomfortable shuffle; a group of Oceanids whispered among themselves and pointed fingers at the Council chairs. Typhon pushed closer, expecting to be called to trial at any moment.

"How do you believe you were called upon by this mortal? It is my understanding that most mortals do not use the offering system anymore." Zeus' voice was amplified louder than before, and it felt like a warning to the room.

Athena cleared her throat. "You are correct. I don't know if she knew that she prayed, as no food was burned or altar built. But I heard her."

Artemis cleared her throat behind Athena and pulled her long, blonde braid around her neck and fidgeted with the tail as she spoke. "I heard her as well."

"And why didn't you respond?" Zeus asked.

"I was helping a few nymphs out in the woods."

Zeus looked around at the other Council seats before nodding once and addressing the room. "The Council of Olympus calls on our witness. The Moirai will ascend the bench; Clotho, Lachesis, Atropos—step forward."

Typhon's jaw dropped as he watched the Fates shuffle out from behind the pillars. All three goddesses still wore their disguises from the mortal realm; Clotho appeared ancient, the folds in her skin hid most of her features, and her back was bowed with assumed age; Lachesis presented herself as a young child, but her face was unsettlingly devoid of expression, and lacked any eyes or a very prominent nose. Then there was Atropos. It had been years since Typhon had seen the Fates, and last he knew, the three were still perfecting their take on what mortals looked like, and she had come the closest to achieving it but still wasn't quite right.

Atropos would tower over most mortal men and women. Her skin was stretched thin against sharp features, and though she had eyes, they looked too large for her face.

Whispers broke out around Typhon, echoing his own questions.

"Why did they appear this way?"

"Did they forget they're in Olympus?"

"Do the mortals believe they belong?"

Zeus raised a hand to silence the murmurs before motioning to the Fates to ascend the steps toward the dais that faced most of the spectators.

"Moirai," he said, addressing the goddesses by their proper titles. "We have called you here today to assist in the decision of Athena's fate. You decide the fate of mortals, correct?"

"No," the women spoke in unison.

Apollo snorted, and Zeus looked taken aback. "You spin the threads of their lives, do you not?"

A flicker of annoyance passed Atropos' face that Typhon would have missed had he blinked.

"Yes," she confirmed, but raised a finger as Zeus opened his mouth to speak again. "It is not our decision how the mortals live and end their lives, only when. We do not choose what events may alter their timelines or sway their decisions."

Zeus nodded. "I see. Please clarify for the Council how your role affects the threads of mortal lives, then."

"Clotho spins the threads of life. This is all mortal life, entwined with their essence. Lachesis measures the threads, and throughout the lives, inspects for loose and unraveling strings. And I snip the threads, deciding how long each life is."

"And what of the unraveled strings that you mentioned?" Zeus asked.

Lachesis giggled, and Atropos placed a spindly hand on her shoulder. "Often, threads are smooth when they are pulled from Clotho's wheel, or unwrapped from one of the spools. But sometimes a mortal makes a decision, or a god interferes in their life, and a thread will become tangled in itself or begin to fray. The small pieces that unravel are potential new endings to that life, places where I could have snipped, or where prophecy has linked the thread with another."

"Does prophecy not link all threads of life together?" he pressed.

Atropos nodded. "Generally, yes, but most of their lives are not significant enough to warrant a prophecy about them, specifically. The stray pieces that branch off, the opportunity for chaos, those are prophecies about extraordinary mortals. Or demigods, or lives that gods cause true interruption in."

Typhon's stomach dropped at the way that Zeus' mouth flicked up into a smirk. He finally made his way to the front of the crowd, and he looked to Athena, waving his hand at his side to get her attention—to no avail.

"Thank you for your explanation. I will assume now that the Council fully understands how the mortals' lives might be affected by our intrusions, and how the

Moirai have the ability to see a physical demonstration of this. It is not up to them whether a mortal undergoes extreme duress, or even wonderful fortune, but a combination of prophecy laid out prior to their existence, and our own doing.

"We took on a great responsibility upon creating the mortal realm, and yet some of us feel entitled to treat it as our playground." Zeus' head snapped to Athena. "Over and over again, if I am not mistaken?"

Athena remained silent.

Typhon's mind raced as he took in the scene. He had to do something to help. Zeus was speaking as if he was going to banish Athena. The Fates looked at Typhon as he cleared his throat.

"She was helping where I failed." He nearly yelled, but his words landed dully between the pedestals, and Zeus narrowed his eyes at Typhon.

"You are not a witness in this case." Zeus' words sounded like a warning, and Typhon hesitated.

He looked at Athena, the dejection in her expression, before swallowing and nodding.

"I am. I arrived immediately after the event. And it was my mortal that was affected," Typhon said.

"You were not present while Athena assisted the mortal, and while you ignored your duty to said mortal, your judgment has already been issued. Unless you take issue with the decision, I suggest you remove yourself from this dialogue."

Typhon held Zeus' hard stare for a moment longer before stepping back and melding into the crowd.

"For your repeated crimes against Olympus, Athena, the Council rules that you will be stripped of your power and banished to the mortal realm." Zeus' voice rang out over the crowd as the Olympians began to shout their protests.

Athena's head snapped up, and her eyes widened in horror. "She was attacked by Poseidon!" she yelled. "He will start another war!"

The crowd pressed in around Typhon harder at hearing Poseidon's name, and Zeus stood from his pedestal. "We won't hear any more inflammatory rhetoric in this hall, unless you'd prefer Tartarus." The crowd continued to yell, their cries growing nearly as loud as Zeus' booming voice, as he turned to them. "Further outbursts will be punished!"

Typhon was jostled as nymphs, dryads, and demigods alike shoved their way toward Athena. He briefly met her gaze—full of sadness, but acceptance—before turning and fleeing, as Zeus continued to yell and the Olympians further threw questions and accusations toward the Council.

11

A light tapping on the door pulled Helen's attention from the book in her lap. Her eyes focused slowly as she realized that she had been reading for hours and the sun had long since set. She set her cup of cold coffee on the side table and rose, stretching her limbs and wiggling her legs to bring some feeling back to her toes.

She took her time moving to the front door. There wasn't anyone to yell at her to hurry and not leave guests waiting anymore, and she smiled at that.

"Hi, Mom," June said, reaching out for a hug before stepping back. "How are you?"

"I'm okay, dear. And you? Would you like some coffee?"

June shook her head and followed Helen into the kitchen. The older woman busied herself with the kettle at the stove while she asked, "What's going on?"

June leaned on the counter, summoning Helen's gaze. "I was thinking about Dad after your visit."

Helen fumbled the cup in her hand, and it fell to the floor, shattering. June jumped back and yelped at the loud sound, and Helen's hands shook as she reached for the broom.

"Sorry about that."

June nodded, hand on her chest. "I didn't mean to throw that on you immediately. I think we need to figure out what to do if anyone comes to collect, since they already have, once."

Helen stayed quiet, working to steady her breathing as she swept up the fragments of broken porcelain. Finally, she stood.

"I really don't know much about what is being collected on. He kept to himself."

Helen clenched her fist around the broom handle, and her stomach dropped. Her poor baby. She did not want to be reminded, but

June's comment struck ice into her chest. "I don't think we need to worry too much. I'm sure I could say he just ran off. That we don't know where he is. Running away with a mistress is common nowadays, you know."

June shook her head. "I don't know, Mom, they came for me first. What if you're next? What if Dad has dug himself so far that he's past repayment?"

Helen's hand shook as she emptied the dustpan into the trash can. She had already thought about that. She had thought herself in circles until she took William's emergency revolver and hid it in the pocket of her dress. She wouldn't go down without a fight. She turned back to face June.

"What do you suggest we do? Go to the police? Are we even sure what happened? Not to mention, the police are tied up in gambling rings here anyway."

June shrugged. "Let's start with the office."

Helen hesitated. "I don't go in there. He gets angry."

"I think we have to. We don't know what else he could be hiding," June insisted.

Helen pursed her lips before gesturing for June to lead the way.

The door to William's study swung open easily, revealing a span of shelves lining the back wall and a desk in the middle of the room. Helen took to one side and June the other, and they opened the top drawers in tandem, pulling out sheets of paper and rifling through in silence. After a few long minutes, June cleared her throat.

"Look at this."

She passed the paper to Helen, whose face drained of color. Along the top in red letters were the words *Overdue Collection*. The statement that followed was unbelievable. Fifty dollars on one line. Thirty on another. One hundred and twenty! No, this couldn't be. She scanned the page front and back before her eyes snagged on the heading. "Whittaker Associations and Loans," she read out loud.

June cocked her head, and her expression was unreadable. "That makes sense. How much is the total?"

Helen swallowed hard. "Over a thousand. Overdue as of last month."

June leaned back on her heels and exhaled.

Helen turned back to her drawer and continued searching. Nearly an hour ensued that way, the pile of debt notes becoming uncomfortably high on the desk.

"Five hundred here."

"Two fifty."

"Another thirty."

"I think I'm going to be sick," June muttered.

A light tapping on the door startled Helen, and she stood quickly, almost prepared to see William standing there with a belt hanging in hand. She breathed a sigh of relief as her eyes focused through the dim light on Ty's familiar form.

"Oh, Ty, I'm so glad you're here." She hurried over and gave him a quick squeeze around the middle. When Helen pulled back, she caught the tail end of a cold look shot his way by June, and she pursed her lips. Ty had always been like an uncle to her daughter; that was not a normal reaction.

"What are you ladies up to?" he asked politely.

Helen swallowed. "Well, William isn't around . . . so we are trying to figure out a debt situation."

Ty nodded and raised an eyebrow, looking at June, and Helen's gaze passed between them as the air thickened. Finally, she blurted out, "What is going on?"

June sighed and stood. "Nothing, but he knows already, it's okay."

Helen took a deep breath, and her stomach twisted. "Thank the gods." She turned to Ty. "I don't know what exactly it was, but he's gone. We are trying to figure out how to keep anyone from finding out . . . and why Don went for June."

Ty nodded. "We'll work it out. What are we looking at so far?"

Helen swallowed hard. "At least three thousand dollars, just from two drawers."

Ty let out a low whistle. "Ouch."

Indeed.

12

The cold night air brushed against June's neck and sent a shiver down her spine as she walked, and she quickly flipped her collar up to protect against it. She should have grabbed a scarf before she fled her mother's house, but she'd felt suffocated, and she couldn't be bothered turning back or running to her apartment.

She stuffed her hands in her pockets, and her finger grazed the corner of a paper. She knew that she should try and find some hint as to what might happen to the house first since William owed such a large debt and was now gone. Though, it was hard to focus on the task at hand, as the letter stashed in her pocket niggled at the back of her mind.

She hadn't mentioned it to her mother, instead choosing to slip it into her dress while Typhon reassured Helen that surely some of the debt would have already been paid off. The handwritten note on Don's letterhead contained an array of threats and intimate details of how Don planned to kill William. It made her wonder if she'd saved her father from an even worse demise.

A brisk walk up the avenue was exactly what she needed. As her blood pumped and her cheeks flushed, she felt warmer and lighter. It wasn't healthy being cooped up, around dead people or otherwise.

She still couldn't believe what she had done; she wasn't a violent person, and the fact that she'd flown into such a rage made her skin crawl.

June directed her thoughts away from her murder as she walked toward Central Park. Thinking about her dad and how different he was near the end draped a sense of nostalgia around her, and she wondered about her mother. How would Helen keep the bills paid now that William wasn't around? She shook her head. Her mother was resilient and would figure it out.

But June? She would have to shoulder what was left by William. It was her fault he wasn't around to deal with it, after all. She would be strong enough for both her and her mother.

A sudden gust of wind blew up the back of her coat, and she wondered about Typhon. They hadn't really spoken since he took off during her rage, barely exchanging glances through the search of William's office. She wondered if he was mad at her for her reaction, or what she'd done to William. Should she be mad at him? Really, this whole thing could go back to being his fault . . . right?

Her thoughts were interrupted as a car slowed and passed her. She turned to watch it drive in a U-turn and park along the side of the road close behind her. She hesitated for a moment before continuing her walk, but when she was halfway down the block, she heard the car's engine start again.

A shiver ran up her spine, and she turned to the southwest corner of the park before it could follow her, but a scream in the distance froze her in her tracks.

"No, stop!" The words rang through the air clearly this time, and June realized it was a woman. Memories of her own cries while trapped under Don flashed through her mind, and she took off at a run, picking up speed as she weaved through trees, crashing over bushes and breaking branches on her way toward the source of the call.

"Help!"

June broke into a sprint, a stitch forming in her side and heart pounding in her chest. She didn't know why she was running toward the scream instead of away, but her heart panged with concern for the woman. She slowed as she neared a walking path in the center of the park, and then she stopped, squatting and resting her arms on her knees. Damn, why didn't she ever take her mother up on the offer to join her women's exercise class? She tried to quiet her breathing, taking big gulps of air before holding completely still and silent for a few seconds. She listened for the call, but when a minute passed with nothing, June began to feel frantic. What if she was too late?

Finally, she heard the woman again. A garbled moan echoed from just a few meters down the path. June strode toward the sound, trying her best to move quickly and quietly so she didn't alert the woman's attacker.

Through a break in the trees, June stopped. The scene she faced nearly made her throw up as the memory of Don's cologne wafted around her. Lying on the ground was a woman, on her back, with her skirt pushed up. Although her stockings were torn and one of her dress sleeves was missing, she was clothed where it mattered. A large man, even taller than Denny, kneeled above her with his knees braced between her legs. With a hand planted on either side of her head, June couldn't make out her face, but after a step forward she realized with horror that the man's face was forcefully pressed to the woman's.

She stepped closer and cleared her throat. The man raised his head and grinned lazily when he saw her. "Oh look, another friend." As he hoisted himself onto his knees, June looked straight at the woman, whose eyes were wide. "Did she invite you to play with us?"

His voice was unsettling, reminding June of the sound a teacher's ruler made sliding across a chalk tray. June forced a smile and nodded tentatively as her mind raced with escape routes. The man's grin widened. He stood swiftly and walked toward her, prowling like a cat that had cornered its prey.

"Oh how fun," he whispered.

He got close enough to touch June before stopping and straightening up. Every instinct in her body screamed at her to run, but she held her ground as he hooked a finger under her chin and raised her face.

"Stop," she demanded.

The man didn't flinch, his finger continuing to trail down her neck. June looked at his feet, and her pulse quickened at the lack of stone. Oh gods, what had she walked into? She whispered the word, and nothing changed. Maybe the power had been a fluke. She was about to go through another attack because she'd been too brave. Too stupid. The man's meaty finger scraped under her chin, and she felt nauseous. She raised her face and met his eyes, holding her breath, scared.

He froze like that—hand held level with his chest and a finger crooked, posture relaxed, face smiling. She watched in mute horror as the last bit of his face faded to a dull gray. Somehow, the marble took out the terrifying air around him. When the last tuft of silky hair on his head was white, June breathed out and stepped backward. There had been no panic from him, no fear. Just the calm of a madman. She almost forgot about the woman as she studied his eyes, until she heard a gasp from behind the man. June leaned around and looked at the woman before rushing to her.

"It's okay!" She fell to her knees, muddying her dress as she slid on the grass. "I won't hurt you. Just him."

Something strange flickered behind the woman's eyes, but the hard look glinting there was gone as quickly as it came, and she let out a gasping sob. "How?"

June held out her arms, and the woman's eyes widened before she fell into them. Her shoulders shook as if she were sobbing, but June couldn't tell if she was actually crying, as a sprinkle of rain started above them.

"I'm not totally sure, but it worked. My name is June, and I came to help."

The woman nodded on her shoulder. It was a long while before she raised her head enough to say, "I'm Sarah."

Sarah pulled back, and the women's eyes met. Something like electricity sparked between them, but June couldn't be sure. It felt similar to when she met Athena. She offered a smile that Sarah returned and was about to ask what she was doing out here when a faint whisper rose from the grass nearby. She strained her neck with bated breath trying to see what the sound was from, and it wasn't until the creature was nearly upon her that she let her breath out slowly. A rather large, black snake was slithering toward her. It reached her leg and promptly wrapped around it, working its way up to rest on the bit of her skirt that sat next to her. She flicked her foot to try and get it off, which warranted a quiet hiss before it curled up. June swore under her breath, and the reptile seemed to wink at her in response. Hopefully, Sarah wasn't afraid of snakes either.

June reached out and touched her shoulder, drawing her attention away from the statue.

"Would you like to come to mine and have a cup of tea?" she asked, keeping her voice steady.

Sarah hesitated for a moment before nodding her head. "That would be wonderful, thank you."

June flicked her ankle, preparing to move, and looked down. But the snake was gone. Maybe she'd imagined it? They rose together, clasped hands, and began picking their way out of the park. As they reached the main road, the woman suddenly looked at the sky and stopped in her tracks.

"I-I'm sorry, I have to go." She let go of June's hand and began backing away, yelling, "I have work tomorrow!"

As she turned and fell into a run, June stood in place, puzzled at the change, before shrugging and continuing on her way home alone. As June walked away from the park, her heart began to thud faster in her chest. She had turned—no, murdered—someone else. She couldn't leave him there, could she? Was there any way to tell that the statues were once men?

Her pace quickened as rain drizzled down, soaking her dress.

She couldn't tell Typhon what had happened; he would have a fit. And it was unfair to place the burden of these strange happenings on her mother.

There was Denny. They'd always been kind and helpful. They had been understanding of the mess she made in the diner, at the very least. She knew that she could trust them, as they had trusted her with her job. Though, she didn't know how they would react to her . . . ability.

13

June chewed her lip as Denny inspected the frozen form of the man from the park. They circled around his left side, leaning in close and squinting at his stone eyelashes.

"He looks very realistic." They turned briefly and raised a brow before looking closer at the man's fingernails. "People are going to ask how you manage."

June twisted her fingers together and swallowed back the unease creeping up her throat.

"I'll say that I've been sculpting since I was a child. And mother is an artist."

Denny made a *tsk* sound and swung away from the statue, fixing their dark gaze on her.

"You're not picking up what I'm putting down, are you?" they asked.

June shook her head before looking at the man again. Sure, he looked a little strange, but still like a statue made of stone. She was sure he could just pass as an exotic marble piece.

"Customers might ask how you made them, so I want to know too. And I want to know how you plan to explain it away so that we are on the same page."

"Oh." June's voice escaped her in a breath, and Denny's eyelids drooped as she chewed her lip once more.

"Show me how you did this," they pressed.

She had only given them the barest details when she ran to the restaurant for help. Something along the lines of "I was attacked, and the man turned to rock and died suddenly," with no further explanation. The last thing June expected was to be asked to explain or demonstrate her abilities.

She shook her head. "I don't know if that's a good idea." As if to accentuate her words, the lights around them flickered.

Denny removed their hand from the gray-washed sleeve of the man and turned to her. "I need to know what I am working with. This is a little out of my realm."

June's stomach dropped at that. They had a point—this was out of both of their realms, and she had come to them for help. She wiped her slick palms down her dress and sighed heavily before looking between the statues. "I feel awful for what I've done, and don't want to do it again, but I also don't know if I can turn anyone else. I'm not sure how I did it." Her voice was small, and as she sat, Denny crouched in front of her.

"These statues have a level of detail in them that I would expect from a sculptor triple your age, Juniper."

Her stomach twisted harder, but she nodded. Before she could say anything, the lights flickered again, and she jumped as a sudden onslaught of rain pounded the windows.

Denny seemed unfazed by the change in weather as they stood and straightened their satin black slacks. "If having the statues here bothers you, we can always put a price tag on them."

She was taken aback, and they chuckled.

"People sell art all the time, I don't think it would be that odd," they said.

"But . . . these are real people," she whispered the words, as if someone might overhear from outside the front door.

They shrugged. "Not anymore. Plus, like you said, both of them hurt you or your family, right? You could also keep the money and use it to pay off some of that debt."

June's head spun as she considered the offer, and the rain and wind pelted at the window pane.

"What about my dad?" she asked.

"Well, did you have a good relationship with him?"

She shook her head before Denny finished asking the question, but stopped to fully consider her answer, then sighed. "I feel guilty about what I did. At one point I adored him, but lately I've been so angry at how he's treated us."

Denny shoved a hand through their already slicked-back hair and shrugged. "Then, what about him?"

June nodded her head slowly. She sucked her bottom lip through her teeth again and looked between the statues before stepping up to examine the fine details of the man from the park once more.

"I would like to see how you do it," Denny said in a voice barely audible above the howl of the wind. "This is unlike anything I've ever heard of."

June touched the cool marble of the man's shirt, ignoring Denny's request again as she slid a finger over a crease in the chiseled fabric. "You really think people would buy these statues?"

"I reckon we could price them at a few hundred a piece."

June's stomach flipped as the lights flickered again, and the rain pounded on the window. She turned to look outside, and as a flash of lightning struck across the sky, a face was illuminated in the downpour.

She dropped her hand and hurried toward the door. "I'll be right back!" she called over her shoulder.

June tied her coat around her waist and looked around just as the freezing sleet hit her face. She had sworn she saw Typhon's face floating on the breeze in the rain, but as she turned around in front of the diner, she saw nothing but raindrops flooding from the sky in front of her and pitch-black night beyond.

"Ty?" she called toward the alley.

"What are you doing in there?" Typhon's disembodied voice spoke from behind her and sent a jolt down her spine.

She spun around and threw a hand to her chest. "Gods, Ty!" As she turned, mouth open to admonish him, where she expected to see her uncle was empty space. "Where are you?"

"I'm here. Where did you get another statue?"

June turned once more before giving up and tightening her grip around her body. "I found him in the park. He was attacking someone."

Silence radiated around her for a moment, and she turned to look toward the window of the diner, where she saw Denny peeking out.

"You shouldn't continue using your gift. Athena's been banished for it, and you can get into serious trouble here. The mortals aren't meant to have gods-gifted abilities." Typhon's voice was low and spoke directly into her ear.

She turned to where she heard him from and wrinkled her brow. "But she gave me the ability to protect myself. I should use it."

"Only if you must."

June chewed the inside of her cheek and nodded before jerking her head toward the window. "Denny thinks that I can sell them. I could use the money to pay some of the debt."

"No."

It was a command, and June turned in time to slam into Typhon's chest as he materialized in front of her. She stumbled backward, and he caught her by the elbow, pulling her under the awning.

"I don't want to watch you go down that path. Trading lives for your own is a dangerous game and will lead to dire consequences. You don't know who you'll hurt," he said.

June searched Typhon's eyes, refusing to back down from his intense gaze. "I asked Denny for help, and that is what they proposed. I think there might be some merit. And these are bad people. William spent the last eighteen years hurting our family, and that man in the park was about to harm that woman just like Don did to me."

The corner of Typhon's mouth twitched down, and he released his grip on her. "Please consider what I'm asking, June. We can find another way. I don't trust Denny, and I don't want you bartering mortal lives in a game against Poseidon."

June nodded. "I'll think about it."

Typhon looked between her eyes once more before a gust of wind swept up behind him and he disappeared in front of her. As she watched the last leaf trail away, she collapsed on the step and hung her head in her hands.

14

The sun beat down on Helen's back, beading sweat in the crease of her neck and in her hairline. She pulled a weed from the soft dirt and threw it to her growing pile of debris before leaning up on her knees and pressing a hand to her forehead. She paused to watch a snake slither through the grass a few feet away, and she watched the sun glint off its dark scales before squinting up at the sky. She hadn't expected it to be quite so hot outside when she decided to work in the garden, and she regretted not grabbing a hat.

As she debated over cleaning up for a break or working through the afternoon, she heard a soft whistle and looked up to see Denny walking past her mailbox. The gold makeup around their eyes reflected the sun like a mirror and made them impossible to miss. Helen sat back on her heels and dropped the trowel in her hand.

"Hello, Denny!" she called with a wave.

Denny stopped in their tracks and peered over the fence. "Oh, good afternoon, Helen. I didn't see you there." They leaned on the gate and motioned at the garden, their smile dimpling their dark cheeks. "Enjoying the nice weather?"

Helen nodded. "I'm a bit late to plant, so I'm preparing for next year instead. Do you walk this way often?" she asked as she stood and brushed stray dirt from her apron.

Denny looked around as if they'd just realized where they were, and Helen laughed.

"I suppose so. I normally let my feet guide me. Would you like to join me?"

Helen looked at the mess of dirt scattered around her lawn before shaking her head. "I would, but I really have so much work to do. Though, I was about to take a break, you're welcome to come in for a sandwich."

Helen swung open the gate, and Denny smiled as she led the way inside.

"Do you spend much time walking?" she asked.

They nodded. "I find it helps me clear my mind when life feels overwhelming. I much prefer it to driving on our roads."

Helen smiled as she removed her gloves. "People drive too fast here."

She was careful to leave her apron in the entryway before she made her way through the living room to the kitchen to wash her hands quickly so as to not drop any dirt that might have made it inside with her.

Denny explored the house at a more leisurely pace.

"This is a beautiful home," they called after her.

"Thank you. We—I've lived here since before June was born." Heat crept up the back of Helen's neck as she scrubbed her arms. She kept forgetting that her husband wasn't around anymore; this was just her house now.

"Who painted the pieces in the living room?" Denny asked from the entryway behind her.

Helen threw a hand to her chest, startled, and turned. "Goodness, you scared me!"

She took a deep breath before letting out an uneasy chuckle and grabbing the dish towel. "Those are all mine. Years ago, especially when June was young, I painted. I haven't put my skills to much use recently, but once upon a time, that was my passion."

Denny leaned against the counter and smiled. "I see where June gets her talent from," they said.

"Yes, I've always been so proud of her," Helen agreed. She looked at the way they bent over awkwardly and motioned to a chair.

Denny was quiet for a moment as Helen stacked meats and cheeses onto the counter. She nearly missed their question as she turned back to the refrigerator for the vegetables.

"And your husband? William? Was he supportive of your dreams?"

Helen made a noncommittal humming noise, unsure of how to answer, or even why they were asking. A fist squeezed around her heart for a moment, and she swallowed thickly as she sliced the bread. He had been supportive, once. Until June was born. Then something inside him snapped and he became a completely different person.

"Yes." It wasn't a complete lie, she told herself.

"It's important to have a supportive partner," Denny said, their dark gaze fixed intensely on her.

She said nothing and continued to make their lunch, and a long beat passed between them before Denny asked, "Where is he now?"

The knife in Helen's hand slipped and smacked into the cutting board. She squeezed the soft flesh of the tomato in her hand a little too hard, using it to steady her shaking and watching as the tiny seeds spilled out.

Denny cleared their throat, and she finally looked up, recovering herself. "I'm not sure. It's been a very difficult time, as I believe he left with a mistress."

Denny's face fell with pity, and they reached across the counter to envelop her hand with theirs. "I'm sorry, Helen. That is truly awful." They leaned in closer, and their voice was as warm as their hand.

Helen's heart skipped a beat, but she fixed her eyes on the tomato, unable to look away as it was smashed beyond recognition beneath her fingers.

15

June strode down the sidewalk with her eyes turned down. She wasn't sure where she was going, but she needed to get out of her house and wasn't due to work until late in the evening.

As she crossed the street, she realized that she was close to Typhon's house and could visit him. When she turned the corner, a loud crash rang out from above her.

"Move!" someone yelled.

June looked up in time to see a flowerpot falling toward her and caught the eye of the man who had dropped it—he stood with his arms just outstretched over his balcony, and his bushy eyebrows were raised. His mouth was still open, about to yell something else, but as June watched him, gray overtook the brown of his skin, and he froze in place.

The ceramic pot crashed down loudly next to her, and she jumped back in shock.

A ripple of fear raced up her spine as her eyes snapped to where the broken shards of glass stuck out at odd angles from the mass of soil, and she glanced back up to the stone man. She looked around the street and found that no one was around, and a wave of nausea roiled through her as she realized what she'd done, before she took off running.

She didn't know where she was heading, but panic flooded her body before she could form a cohesive thought, and all she knew was that she needed to get away. She'd killed again.

She turned a corner, down an alley, and her heel splashed into a muddy puddle. The images of her father and the man in the park forced their way into her mind, followed by the threat of violence against her father from Poseidon.

Her vision blurred, and she found herself at a dead end, forced to stop running, and she sucked in a sharp breath of stale air.

I'm no better than Don, she thought.

Flashbacks slammed their way into her mind, and she crumpled on the ground, choking back tears. She couldn't stop the images from moving in front of her eyes, and the unmistakable smell of his cologne wrapped around her like a blanket, suffocating and slowly choking off her airway.

Tears streamed down her face, and the door snapped shut behind her, forcing the walls of the alley inward. She tried to protest the overwhelming feeling of despair to assure herself that she was okay, but she felt as if she were drowning. Lights flashed in her vision, and a roar filled her ears. The ground rushed up to her, and water from a dank puddle soaked into the seat of her skirt. A voice echoed from somewhere nearby, but it was muffled by her sharp inhale at the cold assault on her skin.

In a flurry of movement, someone in a dark coat ran up to her, crouching and placing their hands on her shoulders. June flinched and screamed, her eyes unable to focus on the person in front of her. All she could make out was a light, golden face and dark shapes under that.

"Hey! Are you okay?" The voice finally broke through the barrier around her, and her eyes focused.

In front of her was a man—around her age, it seemed—with warm, brown eyes and mousy hair that was just a little too long. He wore a dark-gray suit with a navy coat and black scarf. June sucked in a breath as she realized he wasn't hurting her and tried to stifle her tears. "I-I just—" she stuttered, and the stranger squeezed her shoulders and moved to help her stand.

"It's okay. What happened?"

June wiped the salty tracks from her face and steadied her breathing. "Nothing, I'm okay."

Looking side to side, she finally saw that the alley was not closed in, or dark. Two large, clear exits sat on either end, within ten steps. She laughed and hiccupped, her breath ragged from the sudden crying fit.

"I'm okay," she repeated, this time to reassure herself.

The man in front of her gave a look of concern before nodding firmly and releasing her shoulders. "Do you need any help?"

June pulled in a stuttered breath and shook her head. She looked around again, double-checking the ends of the alley. "N-no. Thank you."

Her legs shook as she shoved away from the wall and watched the navy-clad back retreat.

She took a deep breath and smoothed her sweating palms against the wrinkles in her skirt and clenched, then unclenched her fists.

The memory of the flowerpot smashing to the ground struck through her, and she sucked a breath in. She'd done it again.

Oh, gods, no. What if someone else lives there? Or someone sees him?

June hurried around the corner, and upon seeing that she was in front of a café, peeked in through the window. With her face pressed against the glass, she could just see that it had only been an hour since she left home. If the gods were on her side, no one would notice the man until she could get help.

June shuffled anxiously in the middle of the diner, where Denny had asked her to wait while they fetched the man on the balcony.

She looked from the statues already manning corners behind the register and near the door, and chewed her lip. Denny had moved them around, and it made her uneasy. As she approached her father and looked into his eyes, trying to work out if there was any glimmer of blue in them, a key scraped against the door handle.

June jumped back and spun to see Denny's back push in, and she gasped. She hurried over to help them drag the newest stone piece in.

They had to twist and contort him, as his arms were flung outward and his neck craned at an odd angle, and as they each pulled, the door slammed shut and sent one of his feet flying.

Denny and June's jaws dropped in unison, and June scrambled for the limb.

"Can we reattach it?" June asked before kneeling to examine where it had snapped just below the calf. The end of the marbled stone had various ridges that had crumbled into dust, and as she tried to fit the piece back on, more dust fell, answering her question.

Denny said nothing as they dragged the statue farther into the diner. He wobbled on his one leg, and then appeared to stand steady afterward as they stepped back.

June rose from the floor slowly, the leg still clutched in her hands, and they both looked at the statue.

"So, he tried to kill you with a flower pot?"

It sounded more like a statement than a question. "That's what I said earlier," June confirmed.

She had been distraught when she returned and asked Denny for help, but as she tried to think about what had happened with the man peering over the balcony, the exact details escaped her. Was that anger or fear contorting his face? Did he throw the pot on purpose? Yes, he had to have.

"And he yelled at you first?"

June nodded and sucked her lip through her teeth. "I thought before that it was my yelling that was changing them. But that doesn't seem to be the case."

Denny looked around again at the statues and pointed. "They all have their eyes open, but some mouths closed."

Memories of each encounter flashed through June's mind, and she thought of the moment they each started to turn to stone before gasping. "I made eye contact with everyone."

Denny sighed. "It will be hard to avoid looking at people. And if you're going to continue collecting them, we have to do something with them," Denny said, their voice low. "We need to get rid of them."

June swallowed as her stomach turned and acid bit her tongue. "I think you had the right idea with selling them, but I still feel awful guilt. What if they have families that miss them?"

Denny said nothing for a moment, fixing her with their intense gaze as she paced around the diner.

They finally held up their hands, palms to the ceiling, and spoke. "I suppose it's a risk you decide to take. How much do you want to make the money to pay, as opposed to confronting Don, or finding a different option." They motioned at the empty diner. "Three statues do not make a gallery, in my opinion."

She shuddered as she looked at them and remembered watching her father's skin lose its color. "If I am going to turn more, they have to be bad. People who hurt others, like the one from the park. Or my father."

Denny clapped their hands together. "Alright, I'll shuffle things around."

16

Rain pattered against the window at June's back, casting a chill through the city that was abnormal for summer. The café she sat in smelled of fresh pastry and frothed milk, the latter of which worsened her sick feeling, but the atmosphere was so warm that she ignored it, enjoying the sense of security she felt.

She spun her mug around and stroked the handle of it. She had a lot to do to prepare for her new gallery. She felt it was the best option, but both Denny's and Typhon's opinions had made her uncomfortable, and she didn't want to be the villain in anyone's story.

Her train of thought faded as movement down the road caught her eye. She turned her head, and her eyes trailed on a car that looked eerily similar to the one from the park. She breathed a sigh of relief as it rolled past. Only the front was the same, and she wondered at the possibility of being followed. She took one more long look out the window and turned back around.

When she spun her head, she let out a loud yelp, jumping a few inches in the air. Opposite her, where there was previously an empty seat, sat a man in a mismatched gray suit and navy coat. His sandy hair flopped over his brown eyes, and he had a crooked grin plastered on his face as he leaned over the table, mere inches away from June.

Her hand flew up to her heart, and she tried to steady her breathing as she glared at him through the dark lenses of her glasses.

"Can I help you?" she asked tersely.

He sat back in the seat. Removing his hands from the edges of the table, he dropped his smile a bit. He paused for a moment before he jutted his hand out, this time holding it at an angle to shake hers. She looked at him again, baffled by what this man was doing, and placed her hand gently in his and gave it a light squeeze. He looked vaguely familiar, and the color of his coat coaxed the memory buried at the back of her mind, but she couldn't quite place it.

"Can I help you?" she asked again, this time with an edge to her voice.

"I've been following you. I work . . . I mean, I—"

June watched in bewilderment as he blushed.

He whispered, "Let's try again," and snapped his mouth shut, stood, then walked out the door.

She shook her head in amusement at the strange behavior and looked down at her mug for a split second before the bell clanged on the door, drawing her attention back up.

The mismatched man strode back in, scanned the café, spotted her, and waved. "Hey there!" he called.

The patrons nearby looked up at him, confusion clear on their faces. June couldn't help but smile as he stopped behind the chair opposite her and placed his hands on it.

"Hi! My name is Henry." He stuck his hand out to shake hers yet again. She obliged. He pulled back and continued. "I'm an investigator with the police department. May I sit here?" He motioned to the chair, and June's heart rate sped up as she nodded slowly.

Henry sat and leaned forward slightly.

June cleared her throat and asked, "What can I do for you, Henry?" This time, she tried to keep the ice from her tone. Her mind was racing, and bile rose in her throat. She pushed her glasses further up her nose, aware of how intense his stare was, and hoped the lenses would help shield her ability as she intended.

He offered her a smile and stage-whispered, "We're doing great," before straightening up and stating in a normal tone, "Well, Mrs. Georgian, my boss has some questions about Mr. Georgian and his whereabouts."

June's small smile faltered, but she quickly regained her composure. "And what, Mr. . . ."

"Chekov."

"Mr. Chekov, what do those questions have to do with me?"

Henry leaned forward, an air of playfulness still around him. "Honestly, I'm not sure, Mrs. Georgian, but I'd like to find out. May I buy you a coffee?"

June shook her head. "No, thank you. And it's just June. Mrs. Georgian is my mother." She did not need to owe a police officer for a cup of coffee.

Henry nodded his understanding and made his way to the front counter. The second he was gone, June let out the breath she had been holding. Who was this man? Why was he asking questions? She watched as he dug a handful of coins from his pocket and counted a few out onto the counter for the barista. As he gave the woman making coffee another goofy grin, a memory smacked her in the face.

Back in the alley of this same shop, this man had helped her. She knew him, although she'd been so panicked that she forgot his face. She didn't remember him being quite so handsome, though. Then again, she hadn't looked at his face much.

Now he was here to question her. There were only two potential outcomes, she thought. Either she told him the truth and he was so interested in the situation that he'd drop the issue, whatever it was, or she lied and risked him investigating her further.

He returned then, interrupting her thoughts by resuming his seat. "They'll bring mine over soon." June nodded and clasped her hands on the table, bracing herself to come up with answers for him.

He mimicked the movement. "Well, Miss Georgian, my boss would like to know where Mr. Georgian has been. He's tried to see him multiple times with no luck. The man apparently hasn't been at work either." Henry's eyes twinkled as he leaned in and gave June a mischievous grin. "And I would like to know, Miss Georgian, why you are wearing shades inside on such a miserable day. And what you're writing in that notebook." He nodded down at her notes, prompting her to scramble to cover them up, clasping her hands on top of it.

Her mind galloped faster than a racehorse, and her heart felt as if it were going to merge with her stomach. "Well, Mr. Chekov—"

"Henry, please."

"Well, Henry, my father has become indisposed. He's simply not in a state to talk to anyone. I'm happy to answer any questions on his behalf. As for your second question, I'm afraid I must ask one of my own. Do you intend to harm me?"

Henry looked taken aback and shook his head furiously. "Gods, no! I assure you, I am just doing my job. I find you rather intriguing and would only hazard an interest in your . . . quirks. I would never hurt you."

Puzzled, June asked, "Quirks?"

Henry looked a bit sheepish as he explained. "Well, I've seen you around. Part of my job the last month or so has been to follow you. I noticed you doing strange things, and strange things have been happening around you.

"I watched you cart the most interesting marble statue into a diner. Meanwhile, it seems you haven't noticed a massive snake trailing you. Frankly, June, I'm intrigued."

June blinked once at the grin on his face and tried to think of what to say. Icy fingers curled their way around her insides, and her mind raced while moments of silence stretched between them.

June finally cleared her throat and began to move, picking up her book and finishing her tea in one gulp. "Perhaps my mother would be better suited to answer your questions."

17

Typhon shifted to his home in Olympus, materializing just above his couch and allowing the air to lower him. As he hovered, preparing to lie down, an alarm blared throughout the room, and he lost focus, dropping with a painful thud.

"Typhon!" Zeus' voice bellowed above the symphony of high-pitched bells and shrill whistles.

Typhon rubbed the back of his head where it had smacked the arm of the couch and sat up. "What in the realms?"

He shifted back up and pictured the Great Hall, where Zeus was likely waiting for him, and as the wind dropped him with a thud in the middle of the large room, next to a pillar, the whistles pierced his eardrums again.

Typhon looked up to see Zeus standing with Hera and Hestia and lifted his hands to cover his ears. "What is going on?" he yelled over the sound.

Zeus snapped at Hestia and pointed up, and the goddess bustled away. A moment later, the noise stopped.

"We have new rules since the accident," Zeus said.

Typhon's eyes widened, and he looked to Hera, whose expression was bored. Hestia returned a moment later with Artemis by her side.

"Okay, but why did you need the alarm in my home?" he asked, looking to Hestia. As the goddess in charge of protecting Olympus, she had to be the one that had set it in place.

"No one will be shifting to the city directly anymore. Everyone must use the rift, so that we know exactly who is coming in and out," Hera answered. "Every time a resident shifts directly in, the alarms will sound, and Artemis' hunters will be first on the scene."

"We are preparing for retaliation after Athena's banishment," Artemis continued.

"There was such an uproar, and some Olympians followed her. The situation was reminiscent of Poseidon, except she wasn't an active threat against the Council or city."

Typhon raised a brow. "Has everyone been informed? Demeter and Dionysus? Hephaestus? I was clearly caught off guard."

Hestia shook her head. "Everyone who has been here recently. None of them are accounted for, and we can't even be sure of their alignment at this point. Last we knew, Hephaestus was with Poseidon."

Typhon ran his fingers through his hair and looked around the room. A few Oceanids eyed him from a corner, and unease settled in his stomach as he realized that if the news had been passed around about the alarm, they were likely under the impression that anyone setting it off was with their previous figurehead. He turned back to Zeus.

"Do you really think that retaliation will come? Why did you banish her, then?"

"We can't be too careful. It has been a long time since Poseidon's last attempt, but Lachesis implied a change and his growing strength in numbers," Zeus said, ignoring his second question.

Typhon blanched. "Are they still here? The Fates?"

A flicker of annoyance passed over Zeus' face, likely at Typhon's use of the mortal term for the goddesses, but he nodded. "Yes, somewhere."

"Wonderful." Typhon nodded to Hestia and Artemis, who smiled back, and inclined his head toward Hera as well, whose expression remained unchanged, before taking off toward the hallways that wound throughout the city.

He wandered through the streets, asking a few Olympians if they'd seen the goddesses, but had no luck. They weren't in the dining hall, armory, or any of the common areas. As he walked around outside and crossed the bridge into a field, he caught a glimpse of white on top of a hill in the distance.

Typhon shook his head and hesitated for a moment before catching a breeze and landing in knee-high grass beside a trio of women. They were clad in the typical white robes of Olympus, and all looked nearly identical. With long auburn hair to their lower backs, curved noses, and tall, strong figures, the only thing that set them apart from each other was their eyes—all appeared blind, with glazed irises, but they swirled with slightly variant shades of gray.

"So you took your Olympian forms again?" Typhon asked, addressing Atropos.

The goddess turned to him and smirked. "Only for a short time. We'll return to our shop soon, and resume our mortal garb as well."

Typhon shook his head. "You see them every day . . . Why did you never alter your appearance to better fit the mortal realm?"

Lachesis laughed, and Clotho answered, her tone harsh. "Why did you never stop wearing those ridiculous suits? You've consistently been a decade behind."

Typhon's mouth snapped shut, and he smoothed his vest before clearing his throat. "I came to ask a question."

Atropos snorted. "So has everyone else. Do you need to know what quest you're meant to embark on as well?"

"No—" Typhon began, but Atropos cut him off.

"No, no, it's death, right? You want to know when you're dying?"

Typhon looked taken aback, and his gaze flicked between the Fates. "Death? What death? I'm a titan, I'm more immortal than any of you."

Lachesis giggled again, and Atropos waved her hand. "Never mind, then. What is it?"

The unease settled into Typhon's stomach, and he tried to ignore it as he eyed Lachesis. "I wanted to know how much Juniper's fate has changed since her involvement with Poseidon. If there are any events we need to be aware of, or prophecies unfolding?"

Atropos fixed him with a deep stare before sighing heavily. "She is on the exact path she is meant for."

A beat passed before Typhon asked, "That's it? Nothing else?"

"Your lives are heavily intertwined, and if you don't seek your fate, then I shan't give you hers alone."

18

June stood outside of the diner, watching people pass by. An anxious energy prickled down her spine, and her gaze jumped around. She wasn't sure how to choose who to turn next, and the longer she stood around, the more she doubted her plan.

"I could really use your help, Typhon," she mumbled.

As she turned to look down the road again, a large gust of wind tousled her hair, throwing the loose curls in front of her face.

"What's going on?" Typhon asked from behind her.

June jumped, startled, as he emerged from the alley. "When did you get here?" she asked.

"Just now. You called?"

She laughed, but he raised a brow, and she stepped back. "You're serious? You heard that?"

"Of course. It's like a prayer, but stronger since I gave you that blessing."

June nodded and shoved her hands in her pocket before turning back to the road.

"I'm torn up," she muttered, then sighed, glancing sideways at him. He stood back and waited. "I know you don't agree with my plan, but I feel like I need to explore it, but I don't want to change anyone that isn't an active threat, or at least a harmful person."

Typhon was quiet for a moment before he wrapped an arm around her shoulders. "When I pushed you to pursue your dreams of sculpting after school, this isn't exactly what I intended."

"But you'll help me?" June asked, looking up at him.

"Have you considered the house first? What about giving that to Don?" he asked.

June lifted a shoulder. "Mother would still need a place to live, and I also wouldn't put it past William to have already gambled it away."

Typhon turned and stroked his beard. "It's worth pursuing, right? Before selling . . . mortals, right?" he asked, voice low.

June nodded slowly. "Yes, if my mother has her name on the deed, and is able to sign it over, and it hasn't already been taken. But in the meantime, we don't know when he'll come back."

Typhon sighed. "On the condition that you aren't harming any innocent people," he said, with a raised finger, "I think it might be in my best interest to stay on your side, as much as possible."

June raised a brow but didn't ask what he meant, and he pointed down the road.

"If you want to find people like your father, why don't you look in places where he spent time?"

"What do you mean?"

"There's a couple of gin joints down the road, if you look for them."

June's eyes widened, and her face flushed. "How could I get in? Aren't they gentlemen-only establishments?"

Typhon shook his head. "No, since everything has moved underground, you'd be surprised at how easily you'll be served in most."

June nodded. "Okay, I'll head downtown and see what I can find."

"I've got to get going, I have an appointment to make," Typhon said.

June gave Typhon's hand a squeeze and whispered, "Thanks," before he started to spin back up into the breeze. She grabbed his arm quickly, and he stopped, eyes wild and hair windswept. "Can you ask Mom about the deed?"

Typhon nodded and raised his hand to wave, but his fingers had already disappeared in the breeze. June gasped and released his arm, and he was gone in a poof. She quickly shook off her shock at watching him fade into the wind and stepped into a group working their way down the sidewalk.

June walked down an alley, where she saw large barrels stacked outside. She watched as someone stamped out a cigarette and turned to a door tucked between large crates. They knocked in a pattern, waited a few seconds, then twisted the handle and disappeared inside.

She thought that looked like the place she should be going, if she was going to find one at all.

As she walked toward the entrance and wiped her hands on her dress a wave of nausea swept over her, and she had the overwhelming urge to find a different bar. She swallowed hard and pushed forward, rapping on the door, pausing after the second then fifth knock.

A click sounded on the other side of the wall, and it opened a crack before she was let into a dim room. The person leaning on a stool motioned over a maze of crates to another door at the back of the room before sitting down.

June's sickness faded as she wove her way through, squinting to avoid tripping in the near dark, and as she opened the second door, a hum of noise broke the silence.

The room beyond was lit by lanterns at each haphazardly placed table, and a bar stretched across the back wall. The few people scattered around spoke in hushed voices, some holding card or game pieces in one hand and their drink in the other.

No one paid her any mind as she walked around the edge of the room to a stool in front of the bar, including the bartender. She sat down and watched the crowd mingle until a woman slid onto the seat next to her.

"Is this your first time?" she asked.

June started, then shook her head. "No, no, I've been in before."

The woman smirked and pointed across the room to an empty table. "I sit there almost every night. I think I would have recognized you. What brings you in?"

June's mind raced as she looked around. "Just a drink while I wait for someone."

"Not much foot traffic here. Hopefully you're not waiting long." The woman nodded before walking around the bar. June overheard her ask for a rickey and watched her follow the bartender behind a large curtain before emerging again with a drink in hand.

She continued watching the room—a few people left—and as the minutes ticked by, she began to feel anxious about sitting around. The few that approached the bar also ordered before following the bartender through a curtain.

By the third order, June finally leaned over the counter and watched as the man ordering swapped a handful of cash for a small book, then disappeared. Is this what her father had been up to?

She stood and walked to the end of the bar. The bartender said nothing as she waited, and she tapped her foot as he cleaned the back counter. Finally, she tapped the counter, and he turned around.

"Rickey?" she asked.

He snorted and looked behind her. "Are you asking or telling?"

A nerve in her jaw twitched, and she moved back behind the bar as she'd watched the other visitors do. "Telling. I want a rickey."

He threw his towel over his shoulder and leaned on the counter before asking, "Gin or bourbon?"

She hesitated for a moment. She hadn't heard anyone specify. "Gin," she said.

"Alright." He moved to walk behind the curtain, but as it fell, she followed him into a small room. It held another counter similar to the bar with jugs of spirits and tins tucked onto shelves.

"You can't be back here." He turned and crossed his arms.

"I want the special that everyone else is getting." She returned the gesture, and her heart raced as she realized that she hadn't thought this through.

He laughed a short, humorless laugh and pointed at the curtain. "You don't even know what that is. Get out, before I force you out."

"You're paying out on something," June pressed. "I want to know what."

"You need to leave." He moved to grab her arms, and she ducked out of the way, walking to the back of the room.

"What is the money for? Is it for Don?" she asked, voice rising.

The bartender grabbed a glass and lifted it, motioning at her wildly. "You don't belong here. Don't make me use force."

June's heart raced, and she moved out of the way again as he lunged for her. He knocked into the counter and sent a box flying off the shelf as she ducked into the corner, and she glanced down to see envelopes, cash, and what looked like tickets of some sort go flying.

She looked back up in time to dodge another grab, and he knocked her sunglasses to the ground and spun in a daze.

When she blinked away the dizziness and faced him again, their eyes met, and stone raced up his legs, freezing him in place, with his hand outstretched, still holding the glass.

June panicked and looked to the curtain, but no one had come to check on him. She hesitated for a minute before searching behind the shelf. She found a large canvas that she pulled over the bartender to hide him before dragging one of the crates in front of him and running from the room.

No one looked at her as she walked from the bar quickly, and as soon as she was a few yards from the alley, she ran again, aiming for Denny's.

19

Typhon coasted down with a flurry of leaves into Helen's front yard. He slammed down harder than expected, feeling unbalanced after June's interference in his shift. He straightened, pulling his cap down over his forehead, and looked at the house. Whenever he'd visited here throughout the years, it always held a dark air—as if William had bled his anger into the walls, and it had only dissipated once he was gone.

The house's whitewashed exterior was welcoming today as he strode up the steps. He didn't have much time, with an assignment from Zeus to get to.

Typhon reached up and rapped on the door, and a moment later an out-of-breath Helen swung it open. He arched an eyebrow at her disheveled appearance, and she smiled sheepishly.

"Typhon, dear, what can I do for you?"

"I came to ask something about the house deed—on behalf of June." As the words left his mouth, a breeze rustled past him, moving through the barest hint of another gods essence and the hair on the back of his neck raised.

"Oh," Helen breathed, her wide smile dropping. Her brow furrowed, and she looked nervous.

Typhon glanced behind her but couldn't see anything in the dark of the hall. "Am I interrupting something?" he asked, and her shoulders sagged.

"I had a date."

Typhon pursed his lips and nodded, trying not to judge her rebound after William's demise.

"It'll be quick. We just need to know, did Will sign your name to the deed, and was there a witness present? Do you still have possession of it?"

Helen shook her head, concern etched in her face. "He said he did, and the magistrate said he could do it at home and it would be honored by the bank if anything ever came up."

Typhon nodded and smiled.

"Great, thank you." As he began to turn away, a familiar voice carried through the crack in the door before it snapped closed. A shiver ran down his spine as he assured himself it wasn't who he thought.

He shifted in the wind and was gone in a burst of orange leaves.

Typhon pulled heavy wind and rain over Miami. He watched as people walked around the city, to and from work, to the bank, to the park with their children. They all acted as if today was another normal day. Poor mortals.

He didn't particularly enjoy this part of his job. He looked down on the beach as a woman in a light-blue dress tried hard to shut her front gate and protect her flower garden behind it, but the blowing gales kept swinging it open. His brow furrowed. Why did mortals always try to save the most ridiculous things during natural disasters?

He picked up speed as he moved with the wind, bringing water up from the ocean while he waited for Zeus to throw lightning. Normally, once the first strike knocked down a building, people began to realize what was going on.

He had already hit the islands south of here, and he thought that Miami would have been prepared. As he swept up stray umbrellas, hats, and rubbish in his wake, he wondered at the scene playing itself out in front of him. His winds buffeted the sides of houses, and different men and women were working quickly to pull in strangers from the street. A little old woman hobbling with a cane was quickly ushered into a restaurant by a young man in a black suit. Another woman grabbed an abandoned baby carriage and wheeled it into her house.

Typhon worked quickly, trying not to look too closely at the destruction he caused as he tore through the greater Miami area.

Water rose to knee height, and the winds picked up even more.

He'd prefer to spend his time in parks, twirling leaves on a breeze for children to chase. But, sometimes, the population became too hungry and cities became too dense, and disaster was necessary to bring them down.

Typhon grimaced as a house was overtaken by the sea, reminded of a similar storm nearly three centuries earlier. Before Poseidon had gone rogue, he'd been quite helpful with this type of work. He reached out to strike another building and Zeus threw down a bolt on the one next door. Typhon understood the message and threw his arms up, directing the storm higher, faster, and farther across the city. Typhon's blow struck—a wave followed by rain under one-hundred-and-fifty-mile-an-hour winds—and the city went dark.

20

The day of June's grand opening dawned with the sun in the sky and not a sign of rain on the horizon. The gods must be looking out for her, as she threw open her bedroom window and enjoyed the warm rays of light on her face. Maybe Apollo was wishing her luck.

She took her time getting ready. Everything had to be perfect. She stood in front of her mirror, clad in a silken robe, and carefully applied her makeup. She didn't normally wear it, as the colors that were available didn't suit her tan skin well, but today was special. She gently dabbed some cream into her eyebrows, smoothing them down and brushing the hairs in a downward slope, before pressing her eyebrow pencil to the tails to lengthen them. She spit into her cake of black cream and rubbed a brush in it before swiping the flat bristles upward through her eyelashes. A quick line of dark pencil went onto her lash lines.

June carefully applied her red lipstick, making sure not to go outside the natural lines of her lips. While she loved the shape of her mouth, thin lips were all the rage right now. The same color was smudged into her cheeks to finish off. When June stepped back and dropped her robe to examine her body, she frowned at her reflection. The bruises from Don had long since faded, but she swore that she could still see where the marks had been.

She dressed quickly, grabbing a pair of sunglasses after putting on her finest dress, which fell to her shins.

Once downstairs, June moved to make a cup of coffee, but a heavy wave of nausea washed over her as she set down her mug, and she had to grip the kitchen counter to keep from toppling over. She stumbled to the sink, and her dinner from the previous night bubbled up, splashing around the ceramic basin. As she rinsed the sick down the drain, the clock chimed, letting her know that it was eight o'clock. She washed her mouth quickly, hoping that her lipstick was still intact, and snatched up a piece of dry bread to settle her stomach as she ran down to the gallery. There was no time to ponder why she was sick.

June stood in the doorway, looking over her display with satisfaction. Each statue was spaced evenly apart. A few of the diner tables lined the walls in the room she'd been given, and their tops had been covered with a nice, neutral cloth. Plants decorated each surface, including the checkout counter, leaving enough space for people to pay for their art. The kitchen had been converted to accommodate the barista that would arrive soon.

She glanced at her father, who had been placed off to the side, before stepping up to the man from the park and examining him. She'd draped some ivy over him to bring some color to the stark white and dark gray of his new body, and a sign hung around his neck that read *Make An Offer*. A knock on the door tore her attention away.

June flipped her sunglasses down and swung the door open wide to a woman not much older than her. She smiled and stepped in.

"Did you order coffee?" she asked with a chuckle.

June relaxed her shoulders. She showed the woman, who introduced herself as Amy, to the coffee pots in the kitchen and pointed out various things that she may need. Amy assured her that she would be fine to figure it out and got to work setting out sugar and clean mugs.

June returned to the checkout counter to double-check that everything was in place. As time ticked down, she could hear the clamor of people outside the door. She rubbed her hands together fretfully and forced a breath in and out to calm her nerves. Denny should be arriving at any moment, and she was sure that they would have some words of wisdom. But she couldn't help her concerns creeping in.

What if nothing sold? What if she was found out, or Poseidon turned up?

She breathed in and out again. It would be okay.

At two minutes to nine, June glanced at the kitchen before she moved to the front door and plastered a large smile on her face. It was time.

She pushed her sunglasses up the bridge of her nose and swung the door open wide. To her surprise, at least thirty people stood outside. A collective cheer went up, and June quickly composed herself, propped the door open, and began to greet the people as they walked in. All sorts had come to visit—men, women, families with children. Everyone was dressed nicely, and nearly everyone looked surprised to see June standing there. She assumed that they hadn't seen a woman opening a business before. Either way, they were polite as they entered. Things had steadily been changing around here for years, and she hoped she didn't look out of place.

As she was about to go back inside to mingle with her guests, a sleek car stopped in front of the building. Confused, June paused and watched as a chauffeur stepped out of the driver's seat and opened the back door.

Clad in a long fur-lined coat, white stockings, and black heels, the woman who stepped out looked like she belonged on the silver screen. She wore heavy makeup and a head wrap that accented her chin-length coiffed hair beautifully. She smiled brightly at June before stepping past and strutting up to the statues. June felt as though the wind had been knocked out of her and took a moment to breathe deeply again.

As she went about the gallery, speaking with the visitors, she was pleased to hear compliments over and over again on her work.

Mr. Johnson simply couldn't believe the amazing detail in her carvings.

Mrs. Harding was confused that they were all men, but impressed nonetheless.

As the hours passed, people came and went, and June's hope began to fade. No one had put an offer in yet, all seeming to have come just to look. As noon neared, she noticed that the beautiful woman from the nice car was still sitting in a booth, sipping coffee. June approached her and smiled, clasping her hands behind her back.

"Is there anything I can help you with, Miss . . .?"

She held out her hand, which June took and squeezed gently. "Hi, darling. My name is Louise Brooks."

She pointed to the statue of the bartender, who still had his hand raised with an empty glass in it. "Is that one there for sale? I'd love to have him stand in my dining room."

June's heart skipped a beat as she nodded. "Yes, ma'am. Just put an offer in, and I can get the paperwork drawn up."

Louise nodded and thanked her before reaching for a slip of paper and pen from the table next to her. She quickly wrote a number down and folded it in half before handing it to June, who inclined her head, thanked her, and walked to the register.

The air in her lungs whooshed out and tears begin to sting her eyes.

Written in beautiful script on the small scrap of paper were the words *Eight Hundred*. June braced her arms on the counter, breathing hard. Eight hundred dollars? That was more than her wage for an entire year. Oh no, that was too much. She looked up and saw the woman watching her, and she quickly ducked under the counter to grab a certificate to fill out. She took a few seconds crouched on the floor to even her breathing.

Once filled out with the date, sale price, piece number, and a few other details, she took the paper to the woman, who motioned to the man with her. He yanked a stack of bills from his jacket pocket and handed them to June, who, with a look of amazement on her face, curtsied to Louise and breathed, "Thank you, Ms. Brooks."

Louise smiled at her again and rose to leave.

The rest of the afternoon moved quickly. More visitors came through as another wave of them left. She swore she saw the familiar back of a navy coat bobbing about the gallery, but she couldn't be sure.

One more offer came in, for Sarah's attacker. June accepted it graciously, filled out the paper, and carefully tucked the roll of bills into the back of the register.

She began another circuit around the room, her breath catching as she stopped behind a couple. The woman leaned in to her husband, clutched his arm tight, and whispered, "I swear that looks like Daniel. His face is a bit mushed, but look at the pin on his jacket! It looks just like the pin that Macy gave him."

June's breath hitched, and her heart rate picked up as she stepped closer. The man shrugged and grunted, and she clenched her fists in between the folds of her skirt. She stepped beside the woman and cleared her throat.

"Anything I can help you with?" she asked sweetly.

"Oh! No, I think we're okay. I was just saying that this one looks very much like my brother."

The air whooshed out of June's chest, and the walls seemed to move in a few inches as she looked around. Her nails dug painfully into her palms, and she plastered a smile on her face, hoping no one could see the bead of sweat skating down her spine.

"Well, I tend to sculpt based on people I've seen." Her jaw clenched as the woman's eyebrows knit together, and she sent up a silent prayer.

The woman turned back to the statue of the man bending to retie his shoe, his face turned up at the perfect angle, as if he was looking at her to speak.

The woman turned and smiled. "It's just . . . you have such an eye for detail."

June relaxed a fraction, unsure if it was a genuine compliment or if the woman was suspicious.

"My Daniel even had a pin he wore all the time like that—a gift from his late wife." She motioned to the oval disk that sat a bit further out than the man's jacket.

June jerked her chin down, and her stomach turned. She wished Denny was around to intervene, sure they'd prepared the story ahead of time. "Yes, ma'am, I try to capture everything that I can."

The woman's eyes misted over, and June's stomach flipped, stress raging through every muscle.

"It's just a bit strange, as I haven't seen him in over a month. I've tried to visit him a couple of times, but he's been away." She turned back to the statue again and traced her fingers over the broken side of his face. "Odd . . ." she murmured.

June looked around helplessly, scrambling to find something to say before the woman cleared her throat. June turned her eyes up and met a small smile. Where was Denny?

"No matter," the woman murmured, before her voice picked up. "It's just a funny coincidence."

June nodded, shifting her weight to stand partially in front of Daniel. "I'm sure you'll see him soon. I may have just caught a glimpse of him before he left town or something."

The woman reached out to squeeze June's arm, murmuring her congratulations, before moving away.

June sighed heavily and turned to study Daniel herself. She'd have to be a lot more careful in the future. Identifying details like that could really hurt her business. Not that much could be done as far as an investigation goes.

June felt eyes on her back, and she turned, sucking in a breath as her gaze landed on Henry, wearing the same blue coat as before. She cocked her head, and he grinned at her crookedly, offering a small wave before he turned and walked through the door.

She moved to follow him and ask what he was doing, but suddenly Amy appeared in front of her with a mug in her hand. "A celebratory cup of coffee for our artist!"

"Thank you." June tapped the rim of her cup against Amy's. "And cheers to the best help I could have asked for today."

Amy smiled brightly again before scurrying back to the kitchen, and June resumed her walk around the room.

21

As the last person left, June fell into one of the booths and kicked off her shoes, a sigh of relief slipping through her lips. She turned as Amy peeked around the corner and straightened.

"I was going to ask for some help, but you look ill. Is everything alright?" Amy asked.

June nodded. "Yes. I've been a bit sick to my stomach from stress."

Amy pursed her lips, spinning back to the kitchen and disappearing from view, and June heard the clanging of tin and ceramic.

A minute later, Amy returned with a steaming mug. "This should fix you right up. It's a special tea blend of mine and doesn't have caffeine," she said.

June thanked her as she took the cup and inhaled deeply. The smell of mint was overwhelming, but her first sip tasted floral.

Amy smiled and gathered discarded mugs from the countertop before returning to the kitchen.

June stretched as she rose from her seat and set her mug down, then picked her way around the room to straighten chairs. As she bent to collect a lost hat, the bell chimed on the door.

"We're closed," she called.

"That's too bad. I was hoping to chat."

June turned to see Henry leaning against the door. He nodded and motioned around the room. "You do beautiful work," he said.

June's heart rate increased as she realized that Henry was here, and so was the statue of her father. He was looking for William, who was cast in marble just a few feet away—granted, missing half his face. She swallowed and forced her lips to raise into a smile. "Thank you. What can I do for you?"

"I wanted to come and check in. I still haven't heard from William," Henry said.

June turned back to the table and picked up a rag to wipe it down. "I really can't help you," she said.

"You said he was indisposed. What did you mean by that?" Henry pressed.

June shrugged, turning her back further to him. "Really, you should talk to my mother." She glanced over her shoulder before collecting the discarded hat and cloth and walking quickly to the kitchen.

"I haven't been able to get a hold of her," he called after her as she reached the door.

June hesitated. In that brief moment, she considered turning to ask Henry what he meant, but discomfort steered her through the back door to avoid his questions. The last thing she needed was this man gaining any incriminating information from her.

She walked to her mother's house quickly, her heart pounding in her chest. All of the potentially terrible scenarios ran through her mind, forcing her into a jog as she turned the last corner. As she neared, arm outstretched to grab for the gate before she reached it, she slowed her steps.

All of the lights were on in the house, and the car sat in the driveway. Though the curtains were drawn, she could see a shadow moving in the living room.

June hesitated as her hand hovered over the gate, and as a second head popped into view, she pulled her hand back. Did her mother have a visitor?

She stepped away from the gate and chewed her lip, but quickly decided not to bother Helen. This must be why she had missed the opening. The idea of company being more important stung, but June was sure they would get to visit soon.

She tapped her foot for a moment before turning back down the road and heading for Typhon's house. The walk was short, and his presence was always calming.

The overgrown yard and trees that crowded Typhon's small cottage reflected his warmth perfectly. As June hesitated in front of his gate as well, debating if she should really visit, a gust of wind blew past her.

"Hello, June-bee," Typhon said from behind her.

She turned to face his bright, wind-swept hair and tweed suit, and relief flooded through her. "I wasn't sure if you wanted to see me or not. You didn't come to the opening."

Typhon looked down at her and raised a brow before offering his arm and steering them toward the park. "I can't say I am the most pleased with your current plan, but you are an adult, and you can make your own decisions."

They were quiet as they walked together and the minutes passed. Clouds began to roll in the sky, and Typhon looked up nervously.

"We've had such strange weather for summer," June remarked.

Typhon pointed to where lightning flashed in the distance. "It's strife in Olympus, causing change between the realms. Athena's actions triggered a chain of events that I'm not sure anyone was ready for."

"Do I need to be worried?" Anxiety crept into June's voice, and goosebumps prickled across her skin.

"I'm not sure."

June watched as Typhon stroked his beard and stared at the sky across the city with a furrowed brow. She opened her mouth to say something but shook her head and stepped away to give him space. She rocked on her heels and shoved her hands in her pockets, and as she turned to continue down the path, a shrill whistle sounded in front of her.

She looked up to see a man standing a few paces away. One arm was cocked back, and the other was motioning, though she couldn't tell why. As she looked over his face, he began to swing at her, and cold dread pooled in her stomach, followed by a wave of nausea that swept through her body. His hand flicked, turning a small, hard ball in his palm toward her. Her eyes snapped to him as she stumbled back, and stone rushed up his body from the ground to the top of his head in the blink of an eye.

"Juniper!" Typhon called from behind her. He was by her side in an instant and grabbed her by the arm.

"Why would you do that?" he yelled and threw a hand out to point at the newly turned statue.

June hesitated as his grip on her arm tightened, and her eyes widened. He must have realized what he was doing, as he released her a moment later, took a step back, and clenched his a hands at his sides.

"He was going to hit me," June said, quietly.

"Juniper, not everyone is out to hurt you. You should have moved out of the way."

"Look at his arm! He was aiming. My face was right there!" June insisted.

Typhon looked around, and June followed his gaze. The park was empty, but he shook his head. "There has to be another explanation. Maybe he was throwing the toy to someone."

June balled her fists at her sides and glared at Typhon. "I'm telling you, he was about to hit me."

"You have to stop this, June. You can't keep using your power in this way. You're going to become just like Don if you don't get it together."

June's mouth snapped closed. She was unsure what to say, and a long beat passed between them. The sound of voices beyond the trees reached her ears, and Typhon looked down the path before turning to the statue.

"Get control before it's too late," he said over his shoulder. A gust of wind blew over June, and when she blinked, he was gone, as well as the man with the ball.

22

Light dawned through the gray shield of clouds, a shaft of it reaching through a gap in Helen's bedroom window and falling directly across her eyes. She smiled sleepily as she squeezed her eyelids tight against the brightness. She was in no rush to leave her bed.

In the three weeks since William had gone, she felt so much lighter. The fog that had settled over her through years of enduring his abuse was completely gone, and she felt like a new woman.

The company she'd been keeping had helped, of course. Their first date had proven they had much in common, though it was interrupted by Ty. Now her toes curled remembering their most recent night together, and the smile on her face turned wistful. She reached behind her but remembered her bed was empty, and her grin dropped.

Denny had left the day before, insisting they spend a few nights away. An ache settled in her chest as she thought of them.

She rolled to face the space where they had lain in before. Her fingers brushed the pillowcase that she'd replaced on what used to be William's side. A bit of guilt trickled into her stomach, but she bit it back as a frown took over. Sure, she was still technically married, but did it have to be a bad thing that she found good company? She deserved that, right?

The door creaked behind her, and she lifted her head enough to see her new partner stepping in. She smiled and propped up on an elbow. "What are you doing here?" she asked, the early hour making her voice raspy.

They smiled and leaned down to peck her cheek. "I missed you and thought I'd come to cuddle."

Helen smiled and turned back to their pillow, waiting for them to lie down. A heartbeat passed, but they didn't move from behind her. She started to lift up again. "A—" Something dark swooped over her head and cut off her voice. The air turned cold, and dread seeped into her bones. The last thing she remembered seeing as she lost consciousness were a few specks of gold left on the pillow from nights before.

23

June walked down the road toward her apartment, with her arms shoved into the pockets of her coat, staring at the side-walk. She couldn't shake the feeling that Typhon's words had struck in her—a mixture of shame and guilt. She didn't think she was doing anything wrong, just turning men that intended her harm and letting them help her family out of the mess that her father had left.

Her brow furrowed, and she tried to remember if there was anyone else around when she turned the man aiming the ball at her. She was sure she was the only one. He'd definitely whistled at her, and that hard piece of rubber was aimed straight for her face. It could have broken her nose!

She tripped over a raised piece of con-crete and stumbled into something hard. As a hand brushed her arm, she looked down and realized she'd run straight into someone.

"Sorry. Excuse me," she mumbled, swallowing back the anxious nausea that rose into her throat.

"June?" Henry asked.

June's head snapped up, and she met his gaze with wide eyes. "What are you doing out?" she asked before shaking her head. "Are you following me again?"

Henry laughed. "No. I was about to go to eat. You look troubled. Are you okay?"

June smoothed her palms down her sides. "Yes, thank you. I'm just trying to work out some personal issues."

Henry nodded, sending his sandy hair flopping over his eyes. "Well, would you like to go get dinner? We can talk about it."

"Yeah, that sounds nice. I could use some help. Although, it's against my better judgment to confide in the person investigating my family."

June's stomach grumbled as they set out and walked to an Italian restaurant two blocks away.

She noticed that Henry was careful to walk between her and the road, switching sides when they crossed the street. "What's going on?" he asked, leading the way around a corner.

"My family is in trouble."

Henry coughed and cleared his throat before turning to look at her. "Trouble? What do you mean?"

June lifted her head and forced a smile on her face. "Are we friends, Henry? Or is this you investigating?"

He hesitated, clearly uncomfortable. "I thought we could be friends . . ." Henry trailed off and met her gaze.

She quirked her head but began to explain. "A few weeks back, I was attacked at work—by a man named Don. It had something to do with my father owing a debt." She waved her hand dismissively at Henry's concerned expression. "My mother and I did a lot of digging and discovered that he owes thousands of dollars to this one man. With William being unavailable to answer for the mess he's left us in, my boss gave me an idea to earn some extra money

. . ." She paused and waited for Henry to nod, then continued. "Well, I have these two people in my life who mean as much to me as a parent. My boss, who gave me the idea to pay off the debt, is supportive of the idea. But my uncle, of sorts, is against it. He's made me feel morally wrong. But with this threat of Don collecting physically again . . ."

Henry breathed sharply, and June began to tear up. "I worry about my mother too."

The pair went quiet as they waited for a car to pass so they could cross the street. Henry held his arm out to help her across before asking, "Have you spoken to her?"

June shook her head slowly. "No, I haven't seen her in a few weeks, and she missed the gallery opening. I'm sure she was home, but it's unlike her."

Henry chewed his lip. "I wonder if Don has done something."

June startled at Henry's statement. "Do you think he would have already?"

He shrugged. "Think about it. He came to collect a debt from you, right? If that didn't make your father pay, then what next but go after his wife? She wasn't home when I went knocking. Maybe Don plans to use you and your mother both to get to William."

She swallowed hard. "Maybe you're right."

"My boss is a man named Don Whittaker."

June went pale.

"Well, unofficial boss of my boss. I'm pretty sure he owns the department, even though it shouldn't work like that. But he's come into work. I watched him shoot a man once."

June's hand trembled as she raised a hand and touched her neck. Her throat was suddenly dry, and when she took a breath, her lungs felt as if they were punctured.

Henry grinned his goofy grin. "It can't possibly be the same Don, right?" His face dropped as he noticed the look on June's face, and he looked at the restaurant a few steps away. "I don't think I'm hungry anymore."

They stood outside together in silence, backs lit by the warm light cast out of the windows behind them, and he turned to her.

Henry finally spoke, startling her. "Maybe you should go to his work. Your father's, I mean. They may have an idea of where all his money was going and the extent of his relationship with Don. It was the manufacturing plant, right?"

June nodded slowly, a chill traveling up her spine.

"They won't let just anyone in. I'll sneak in and borrow a uniform for you." He smiled, and June thanked him.

"But why would you help?" she asked.

He shrugged. "Consider it my civic duty. I'll go tomorrow." Henry reached out a hand to squeeze hers.

He opened his mouth to speak, but his sentence was cut off and hand torn away from June's as someone squealed, "Henry!"

Wind knocked out of her, June straightened and rebalanced herself before looking at the woman now standing with her arms wrapped tightly around Henry's neck. He had crimson cheeks and held one hand out, hovering over the woman's back, as if he was unsure whether or not to return the embrace.

June cleared her throat and spoke. "Hello . . ." She trailed off as the woman turned. She wore a long fur-lined coat, and her hair was curled in an updo. When June saw her face, she laughed in disbelief. "Sarah?"

Henry looked confused. "This is Eris," he said blankly.

The woman laughed, looking back and forth between them. "Oh goody, my boyfriend and my hero are in the same place."

June swore the confusion on Henry's face matched her own, but she blurted out, "Boyfriend?" At the same moment Henry asked, "Hero?" They exchanged a look that further deepened the red in Henry's face.

June stepped forward to address Sarah, who still had an arm around Henry's waist. "I thought your name was Sarah. That's what you told me in the park."

The other woman shrugged. "Sorry, I lied."

Irritation skittered up June's spine as she watched Eris reach up and try to kiss Henry, who turned his face away. June cleared her throat loudly, and Eris finally let go of the chokehold she had Henry in and spun, planting her hands on her hips. "Yes?" She raised an eyebrow, as if June was intruding on her night, and electricity crackled between them.

June's anger flushed her skin. "Henry would not have asked me to dinner if he was seeing someone."

A look of pure rage crossed Eris' face before she smoothed the front of her dress and smirked. "I'm sure he didn't think it was a date, anyway. We were just out together the other night, after all."

June looked at Henry for some explanation, but he just blushed darker. She glared at Eris' back as the woman snaked her arms around Henry's neck again and leaned up. June didn't stay to watch the kiss she planted, instead turning and stomping down the road toward home.

24

June stood in the middle of the gallery as the sun set, broom in hand, staring blankly at the man from the park. As the memory of Eris crept into her mind, she reached a finger out and traced a marble vein down his face. She didn't understand how Henry could skip telling her such a vital detail, but as she pondered, a sound from behind her made her freeze. She gripped the broom with both hands, prepared to swing it at whoever was there.

"Well, well, well, Juniper, what in the realms has happened here?" A deep, silky voice echoed off the statues.

June spun quickly, trying to locate the source of the noise.

June stuttered out, "Who's there?" and inched toward the front door, ready to run.

The intruder laughed. The sound was warm and pleasant and reverberated around them. "Don't you know, girl?"

June spun again and found herself face-to-face with Denny, though something about them was different. "Denny? Where have you been? And what are you wearing?"

They wore the strangest black suit. Stiff and shiny, it appeared to be made from the skin of an exotic reptile. Even their shoes were scaly. *Regal* was the only word that June could think of to depict the picture of elegance standing in front of her.

They bowed deeply with a sweeping motion. "My name is Asclepius. Pleased to make your acquaintance." They raised their head, and their eyes twinkled under an arched eyebrow.

June gasped as she noticed the faint buzz around them. It felt as though the air was charged with static, which she had never noticed before.

"You have the same feel around you as Ath . . ." She trailed off, realizing that Asclepius wouldn't know what she meant.

But it seemed that they did. They nodded, and a grim expression flickered over their face. "Dear old Athena. She was banished and had her powers taken for crimes against Olympus, you know." They gave June a pointed look, as if it were her fault. They waved their hand airily. "Nothing to concern yourself with. You're hardly expected to know the rules."

She chose to ignore that. "How do you know all of that?"

Suddenly Asclepius spun, and their body seemed to fall in on itself. As they moved, the scales on their shoes climbed, melding together with the strange black suit. The scaly sheath writhed and twisted together, and a slithering sound filled the air. After a few seconds, a large and familiar-looking snake with black scales that flashed gold lay coiled at June's feet. She gasped loudly and threw her hands to her face while Asclepius sprang back up from the pile of scales and yanked the collar of their suit jacket back into place.

June sank to the floor, exhausted, trying to wrap her mind around what she just saw. Her boss, and primary assistance in all this trouble, was a god. She placed her head in her hands and fought back a wave of dizziness.

"I'm formerly the God of Medicine, if you need the formality," Asclepius winked.

"What do you want?" she muttered.

Asclepius seemed not to hear her question as they stepped up to the man holding a toy and looked at him.

"Who do we have here?" They looked at June with a raised eyebrow.

She looked up, dropping her hands. "He almost hit me with that ball."

"Why would you change him?"

June blanched in response. "I had to! He could have killed me!"

The god's eyebrow went up farther, and they pointed to Daniel. They gave her another look, and her confidence wavered. She didn't have a good reason for turning the man who had been tying his shoes. She thought he might have tried to look up her skirt, but she knew the moment it happened that it was a flimsy excuse.

Asclepius circled the man once before speaking. "Us immortals can't stop the stream of time, you know. We simply ride it. Let the Fates weave what they will. You should too, but here you are . . . interfering more in human lives than any god."

"But I have the power to stop bad people. I should use it."

They whirled on June. "No, you shouldn't," they hissed, stepping closer to her.

She held her ground and lifted her chin defiantly. "Maybe I just have better morals than you."

The god narrowed their eyes. "Oh, honey. You think you're so special? You're not. You look at the clouds floating by and see them as wisps. Don't you realize that even though they have the power to give life through rain, they also hold the power to snatch it away just as easily? Should they do that every chance they get? What would happen to the world if a torrential downpour took hundreds of lives every day? Everyone has power to some degree. Even fragile girls caught in the wrong place at night. It's how you choose to use your gift and knowing when the right time is."

June tried to protest "But Athena—"

"Tsk. Athena didn't give you some wonderful power or terrible curse. She simply opened your mind to the possibilities that already lay within."

Asclepius walked away, rounding each of the marble statues scattered about and looking at them. "Don't you see? You have become the very danger you feared, simply by using that power every chance you can. Look at all this destruction!" They spread their arms, and June's eyes widened as she took in the men standing in different places with pieces of their bodies missing. It was as if she was looking at the room with completely new eyes.

The golden god paused for a moment as understanding dawned on June. Then they pointed at the man with the ball. "He was a father and was expecting a second child. He meant you no ill will, and he was whistling to his son to catch the ball."

Asclepius approached the flowerpot man, studying his face closely. "This one accidentally nudged that plant off the sill. He was trying to catch it when you killed him."

They turned and faced June, hands on their hips. "Don't you see? Not everyone meant you harm. You simply took their words, or expressions, or body language, and magnified them to turn them into a villain in order to justify your own actions."

June stared at the god, shock overtaking her features. Her mind went blank as Asclepius chuckled. "You're playing with fire, girl, involving yourself in things you don't understand." Their eyes narrowed. "Maybe you should focus less on murdering men in cold blood and more on your mother."

On finishing their last, snarky comment, the god collapsed back into snake form and promptly disappeared into thin air.

25

A stitch formed in June's side a block from her mother's house, and as she took a wheezing breath and leaned over the fence, bile rose in her throat. Exhausted from her run, she couldn't keep it down this time, and vomited into the garden bed. When she finally straightened, she rubbed tears from her eyes and pushed the gate open. The hinges creaked loudly, cutting through the still air. Mother hated that sharp sound and usually kept the gate well-greased.

The house was dark and there was a pile of mail on the porch. June continued up the steps, pausing to knock. No answer. She tried again, louder this time, and waited, ear pressed to the door.

There was no movement on the other side. She tried the door handle and was surprised to find it unlocked. Her mother would never leave it that way. She took a tentative step into the entryway as the hinges groaned and the door swung open. She jumped when the handle tapped the wall behind it.

"Hello?" Her voice echoed down the hall. No response came.

The sudden terrible image of her mother dead on the floor flashed through her mind. She tried to shake it out, and blood spattered around the picture before it faded. Nausea rose up, and she swallowed hard, trying to ignore her nerves running wild.

She froze when she stepped into the living room. The blanket and small pillows that normally decorated the couch were thrown across the floor. The inner curtain on the massive window facing the road was torn. The corner of the rug was turned up, and her mother's favorite family portrait was askew on the wall. Knickknacks that normally lined the fireplace mantle and small side table were knocked aside as well. June sucked a breath in and went to the kitchen, where she found a similar state.

Dishes were shattered on the floor. Cabinets were flung open. The hand towel was in the sink. As she slowly walked through the kitchen, she was relieved to find there was no blood, although there had clearly been a struggle. The dining room was untouched, save for a chair that her mother must have been sitting in. June carefully tucked it into place and ventured back down the hall toward her parents' bedroom.

Before she could open the door, a rustling sound filled the hallway, and she spun quickly, ready to swing at whoever was there. She let out a loud sigh of relief as Asclepius materialized in front of her. The relief turned to annoyance and then irritation as she noticed the wide grin on their face.

"What? What are you doing here?" she hissed.

The god stepped away from the wall they leaned on. "Is that any way to greet a friend?" They moved to walk past her and into the bedroom, but she stepped into their path.

"I wouldn't call you a friend right now."

They raised their hands in mock surrender and stepped back, allowing June to stick her head through the doorway. Everything was normal there.

"I'm trying to help. You've been unfocused."

June whipped her head around and glared at them. "What do you know? Why are you here?" She laced her words with as much venom as she could muster.

"Oh, nothing."

The ice in her eyes did not thaw as the god walked into Helen's room and stepped up to the wide vanity opposite the bed, tracing the hand-carved edge with a gold-tipped nail. They turned and smirked at June.

"Nothing happened *in here*, per se."

June forgot their size difference in an instant and descended on the god, reaching up to grab the collar of their suit and yanking them down to eye level. Asclepius quickly transformed, but that forced June's hand to tighten around their neck. Their slitted eyes bulged, and they popped back into human form, now bent at an awkward angle and nearly nose-to-nose with June.

"What . . . happened . . . snake?" She was seething, rage making her voice shake, and she squeezed Asclepius tighter and tighter. Finally, they threw up their hands again, coughing and sputtering when she released them.

"Okay, okay." They breathed unsteadily. "Yeesh, you're stronger than you look."

June fixed them with a glare, and they stepped back.

"Someone took her."

"Who?" June demanded.

Asclepius raised their hands farther, wincing at the tone in her voice. "I can't tell you exactly, but . . ." They chuckled uneasily.

Confusion bled into June's anger, and she continued glowering at the snake-turned-person.

"She didn't go down easy."

June thought they sounded a bit de-ranged for a moment, and she raised a brow at them.

"From what I could hear," they added hastily, shrugging and straightening their jacket. June followed their gaze to the ground, where a crumpled handkerchief was discarded on the floor. "Guess we know where you get that fire from."

The memory flooded her mind of the night she met Poseidon, the dark, almost black, navy suit he wore and the matching silk square. June promptly turned and stormed from the room. Asclepius ran after her to yell, "Wait, where are you going?"

She ignored them and kept walking, leaving the house and breaking into a run down the street. How dare Poseidon come for Helen after what he'd already done to her! Tears stung her eyes as she ran, heart pumping hard and blood rushing in her ears. How could he think he could get away with this?

She was going to get her mother back, and get rid of him, if it was the last thing she did. Her stomach felt as if it were climbing into her throat as she broke into a run, and as she turned the corner, she hit something hard. Her vision faded as she fell into darkness that pulsed and swirled with stars.

June cracked her eyelids open and tried to lift her head, but a wave of nausea rolled over her.

Fragments of a dream faded as her vision cleared. The marble dais she'd seen was replaced by the hospital bed she laid in, and she was vaguely aware of Henry's hands on her arms, holding her up as he guided her somewhere. He said something, and she was whisked into a small room. The smell of chemicals filled the air and helped clear her head, and she looked around to try and get a bearing on where she was. She couldn't remember lying down, but a thin bed with a metal frame and stark white sheet was underneath her. A flimsy chair sat next to her, with a cloth-covered table and mirror across the room. Her skin was clammy, and as she raised a hand to wipe sweat from her forehead, it shook.

Henry paced nearby, concern clear. Finally, a doctor appeared in the doorway. June couldn't make out their conversation as they carried on in hushed whispers, but by the time the doctor disappeared again, she was starting to feel more normal.

Henry crouched by the bed and reached out to hold her hand, stopping as she looked at him and pulling back after grazing her fingertips.

"How do you feel?" he asked.

"I think I'm okay." Her throat was sore, and her voice sounded hoarse. "Why are you here?"

"You ran into me," he explained. "When you fell, I think you hit your head. But the doctor's said they wanted to check you out."

She grimaced. "I'm fine, really."

Henry did not look convinced, and he gazed at her with something unrecogniz-able in his eyes. Before he could say any-thing else, a nurse shooed him out to make room for the medical staff. A doctor walked in carrying a tray with all sorts of tools and cups, and after he placed it down, he asked

June some questions and poked and prodded her. She did as she was instructed, and as she tried to walk upright and return to the bed, another wave of dizziness and nausea washed over her. Henry returned as soon as there was space in the room, and he held a tin bucket for her as she leaned over the edge of the hospital bed and retched. Thankfully, nothing came up and the feeling subsided quickly.

The pair sat together in terse silence in the hospital room. June tapped her fingers impatiently against her leg, anxious to leave and search for her mother. She thought of bringing up the empty house to Henry—he had been looking into her family, after all—but she didn't know where he stood anymore.

She considered asking about Eris, to break the silence, but wasn't sure how to bring her up, either. So they continued to swap uneasy glances.

Finally, the doctor came back to release her. He promised he would be in touch soon with an answer to her problem.

As Henry helped June climb into his car, she stopped, examining the side of it. She turned to him upon realizing where she recognized it from.

"You were the one following me!"

He looked taken aback and peered around as if searching for help before responding. "I told you that," he said slowly.

June, dumbstruck, leaned back in her seat and let him close the door.

He had, indeed, but for some reason, she hadn't connected the car with Henry. That meant that he was there from the beginning, when she had helped Sarah— Eris—in the park.

Henry took his place at the steering wheel and threw a glance her way before starting the car and driving back to June's apartment.

They were silent the entire way, until he parked in front of the gallery and moved to get out and open her door. She shook her head. "It's okay, I can do it."

She climbed out of the car and hesitated before saying, "Thank you," and following him to her front door.

As she walked to her room, she realized how anxious she was to get into bed. Her body felt heavy, and her mind even more so. She thought that perhaps some sleep would settle her nerves and sickness. Then she could find her mom and deal with Poseidon.

26

Typhon floated on a wind current outside of the diner, watching as a car pulled up to June's apartment. She opened her door, but Henry ran around quickly, and they had a short standoff as June attempted to get out on her own. A voice below Typhon laughed. He looked down to see Asclepius lounging on a vine, and he hesitated. He hadn't seen the god in years, since they started masquerading as the mortal Denny.

Finally he said, "Young love, eh?"

Asclepius hissed a laugh, "Indeed."

They watched together as June walked toward her apartment. Henry opened her door and leaned on its frame to say something. She smiled up at him, and he offered her a hand up the step.

Typhon sighed. "I suppose I'm not need-ed here anymore. He protects her well, for a mortal."

Asclepius' tail twitched. "You should con-sider rejoining us in our fight."

Typhon said nothing for a moment. "I never wanted this fight."

Asclepius flicked their tongue and bobbed their head. "None of us did."

"You've clearly chosen your side, though," Typhon snapped, spinning around the vine angrily. "You disguised yourself just to get close to my girl."

"You have to do what you can to survive."

Silence stretched between them as they watched June and Henry. It took everything in him not to reach out and strangle the snake. Asclepius had never truly done any-thing wrong. It's like they said—effort to survive—but Typhon was suspicious of their hanging around June, and everything they did for her with nothing in return.

"You know, she's likely the key to ending it all." Asclepius' words interrupted Typhon's thoughts, and he spun to look at them.

"No, she couldn't be. She wouldn't survive."

Asclepius flicked their tongue. "You never know. She could save us all. Prevent the inevitable war."

"I'm more worried about the fact that she has caused so much change between the realms. I'm not even supposed to be here."

Typhon turned back to the window and watched for a moment longer before drifting away. Maybe Asclepius was right.

His breeze took him up over June's apartment and across town, clear to Eris' house.

27

Bright light blinded June and she squinted against it. It took a moment for her eyes to adjust before she realized that it was actually the sun shining down on her. She was confused, as she could swear that she had just been in bed, and looked down to examine herself.

She was dressed in a strange white robe, tied in place at her waist with a golden braid. The skin on her arms looked fresh, glowing even, and there was no trace of the nervous sweat that had been coating her body earlier. In fact, she felt amazing. No knots in her stomach, no anxiety riddling her brain. She looked around and was surprised to see that she was standing in a large marble room. Gray veins formed intricate patterns in the glossy white surface, and columns lined the walls. She raised her hand to shield her eyes from the sun and looked up to see a gilded ceiling, with a hole cut out to let in the light. It shone directly where she stood.

She stepped to the side and looked around again.

"Welcome, young one." A voice behind her echoed around the chamber, and she spun to see a handsome man step forward. He looked old enough to be her grandfather. She felt calm, and she smiled at him.

"Hello," she said pleasantly, her voice coming out easily.

The man walked toward her and held out his arm, which she graciously accepted. They walked around the room slowly, her hand on his upper arm. As they walked in silence, she studied him. He was the same height and build as Poseidon, but he appeared much older. With a grizzly gray beard sticking out at odd angles, and short graying hair to match, his eyes were the shade of rain clouds before they threw a storm down over the city, and they seemed to swirl like clouds too.

As they approached a doorway, the sound of a waterfall filled the air around them, and they stepped out onto soft green grass. Butterflies and other insects flitted here and there, and the sun shone radiantly against a bright-blue sky.

"Where are we?" June finally asked.

The man simply smiled and continued leading the way over a small wooden foot-bridge. He suddenly looked at her as if he'd remembered something. "Congratulations on your exciting news!"

Puzzled, June stopped. "What do you mean?"

The man with the gray eyes looked down at her stomach. She looked down, and, suddenly, where there was nothing before, June now held a bulging bump. It was as if she had become eight months pregnant in a matter of seconds. Horrified, she looked back up to ask what happened, but the man was gone.

The bright colors around her faded, and a loud booming sound echoed from the horizon while the grass and water around her melted from under her feet. She began to fall, her scream caught on the wind that blew up past her body as she fell through dark space. She wasn't sure if she was screaming because of the pregnancy or because of the fear of going *splat* on the ground, but it was torn from her by the torrential wind anyway.

Thick black streams of stars passed her in a blur, caressing bits of her free-falling body as she was thrown down. She twisted and turned through tendrils of ink until she could see herself falling toward the slowly spinning Earth through the billion points of light. It came closer and closer until she could almost make out the buildings of New York. She squeezed her eyes shut, bracing for impact.

"June!" A loud banging sound woke June with a start, and she quickly sat up, her dream fading fast. She tore back her blankets and looked at her stomach, sighing with relief at the lack of a bump. She crawled out of bed and slid her feet into slippers before running downstairs.

Henry called her name twice more from behind the door before she reached it and swung it wide open. He nearly tripped over the entry and grabbed the doorframe to balance himself.

She gasped as she looked at his face. One of his eyes was swollen shut and colored a sickening shade of violet. His lip was missing a slice from it, and blood trickled from his right ear. His typical white button-down was torn at the collar, and his coat was nowhere in sight, although he held a tight bundle of dirty blue cloth in one hand.

"What happened?" June asked as she ushered him in.

He grinned sheepishly and shrugged. "Lovers' quarrel?" he offered as he stepped past her and went to the dining room.

June snorted a laugh of disbelief and stopped in front of him. She looked him up and down once more before pointing at a chair and saying, "Sit."

He obeyed, and she got to work making him breakfast. She grabbed some eggs from the basket on her counter and vegetables from the fridge, and as she chopped mushrooms, Henry explained.

"I went to the plant like we discussed, but for some reason, Eris was there. She beat the living hell out of me for embarrassing her." He rubbed the back of his neck and looked up at June before placing his hands on his knees, palms up. "I'm sorry."

She stiffened. "What for?" She tried her best to sound as if nothing had happened. She carefully cracked two eggs in the pan and added a handful of mushrooms and tomatoes before taking a spatula and breaking the yokes open, perhaps a bit forcefully.

"I should have told you. I did take her on a date, but it was over a month ago, and I hadn't seen her since. I didn't think anything of it because we weren't really seeing each other."

"You don't owe me anything. We only went to dinner as friends."

"I'd like to take you to dinner, at some point," he replied.

June nodded, tension in her shoulders giving way to relief.

She mentally kicked herself for caring so much when they had only properly met a few days before. She flipped the omelet out of the pan and took the plate to Henry, stopping a foot away. He still looked apologetic, almost as if he was waiting for her to yell or hit him. She set the plate down gently and squeezed his shoulder.

"It's okay." She caught a glimpse of a smile breaking across Henry's face as she moved to serve herself.

"How are you doing?"

June stepped back as she said, "Good, I think. Thank you."

"I brought the uniform you'll need." He set the bundle in his hand on the table and clasped his hands behind his back. "And this envelope from the hospital was out there as well."

28

She went upstairs and dressed quickly, then donned one of Ty's driver's caps that he'd given her as a child, careful to tuck her stray curls up into it. She pulled her sunglasses on and slid her feet into an old pair of her father's work boots. They were at least four sizes too big, but she hoped that would lend to her looking like a man. After she took a few steps, she grimaced and slid her feet back out, taking a moment to hunt down spare stockings from around the room. She stuffed them into the toes of each boot, so they weren't so clunky and loose, and tried again.

When she returned downstairs, Henry was gone, but she was pleasantly surprised to see that he had cleaned up the breakfast dishes and put away the leftover food. She couldn't stop to appreciate the gesture for too long, though, as she had to move quickly.

She left the house and strode down the sidewalk with purpose, heading for the plant that her father worked at. Thankfully, it was only on the other side of Central Park, about twenty minutes.

As she passed the café where she first met Henry, her thoughts turned to him. The more they were seemingly forced together, the more she enjoyed his company. Clearly, he felt the same, but she hoped it wasn't superficial or wasn't just a way to get answers about her father.

As she passed the park, a slithering sound caught her attention. She rolled her eyes as a large snake began to weave next to her. Its scales were pitch black without the sunlight to change them. "Really, Pius? Not now."

Asclepius sprang up next to her and scrunched their flat nose at her. "Did you just nickname a god?"

She shrugged and kept walking, speeding up slightly to try and lose her new companion. "How is it different than you going by Denny for gods know how long?"

They jogged the few steps it took to catch up, then spun around to walk backward in front of her. "It's different. That's to blend with the mortals." They motioned around at the empty street, as if a crowd was suddenly going to appear. "Where are you going?"

June sniffed. "None of your business. Why are you interested all of a sudden?"

They held up their arms. "Okay, I know I haven't been the nicest, and I'm sorry. I should have told you sooner." Their gold-tinted lips spread into a grin. "There are bigger things at play here, though. Plus, we have history."

June stopped and narrowed her eyes. "What do you mean?"

Pius' eyes twinkled. "You tell me yours, I'll tell you mine."

"Do I still have a job?" June asked.

Asclepius raised their palms to the sky and shrugged. "I don't see why this dispute has to get in the way. I never did enjoy management."

June sighed and began her walk again, and Asclepius fell into stride next to her. It wasn't as if she had an abundance of gods to get information from. Even if Asclepius was a snake, in more ways than one, if they could give her some inkling as to what was going on outside of her small world . . . maybe it would give her a leg up over Poseidon.

"I'm going to the factory my father worked at. I'm going to see if his boss knows anything further about the debt he owes." She turned to demand an answer to her question, but she was alone again. She shook her head and muttered, "Gods," before turning a corner and coming to a halt in front of a large, gray building. The length of six generously sized houses, and twice as tall, it towered over her, casting a massive, ominous shadow. She looked around and spotted a large group of men heading to the entrance of the lot. She jogged to catch up, falling into step behind them.

She managed to slip in with the group undetected, and she tried to keep her head down as she looked around for a manager's office or someone not in a jumpsuit. A man in front of her headed for the back of the building, and she followed, trying to ignore the large machines. She wasn't sure exactly what this plant was even for, but it was huge—and smelly.

She stuck to his shadow until he turned right, grabbing a stack of papers from the wall in front of him and heading for another group of workers ten feet away. She looked up and was shocked to see a door in front of her with the word Office written on it. She tried the handle, and it opened. As she began to walk in, a man yelled from her left. "Hey!" She froze. "No eyewear aside from safety glasses." June dropped her voice as low as it could go and called back, "Sorry," before ducking into the office and exhaling loudly. That was almost too easy.

With her hand still on the door handle, she heard someone clear their throat behind her, and she steeled herself. As she turned, the pair of blue eyes looking back at her sent a cold shock down her spine. "Eris?"

The back of her neck prickled, and the room filled with the same energy that surrounded Asclepius and Athena. It clicked then, why Eris called herself Sarah. Her cheeks heated and she balled her hands into fists as Eris smiled wryly. The goddess motioned to the chair in front of her. "Please sit, June."

June moved to the chair, trying to hide her confusion while not breaking eye contact. "I'm here about my father." Her tone was even, but her heart was hammering at her ribs.

Eris sighed and moved the stack of papers in front of her. All traces of the cynicism and loathing in her expression faded. June looked her up and down, surprised to see that she was wearing a suit. It looked like a man's typical work suit, but it had been tailored to accent her narrow waist. She looked down and saw a name plate that read "Sarah Johnson, CEO."

June hid her discomfort as well as she could and waited for Eris to speak.

"I knew you'd be here sooner or later since your father disappeared. We've all been wondering where he's gone, you know." She looked June in the eye and cocked her head.

June cleared her throat. "He's become indisposed. What are you doing here, Eris? First you're in a park being attacked, then seemingly attacking my date. Now you run a manufacturing plant?"

Eris shrugged. "I'm a woman of many talents."

June slammed her hands on the desk. "Cut the nonsense. I know exactly who you are, and you're going to tell me what my father did to cause Poseidon to seek me out. He spent most of his time here. What happened?" She gritted her teeth, and Eris crossed her arms and raised an eyebrow, nodding at the chair. June breathed in heavily to try and calm the rage boiling in her chest before resuming her seat.

"I can't tell you the extent of your father's issues. I don't even know. I was his boss before getting involved in your life. But I can tell you two things. First, he hasn't been here in a long time." June scoffed. "Second, he took out a lot of advances before leaving with no notice. He owes me a lot of hours, or a lot of money. Either of which I would be happy to collect on." Eris sighed at June's glare again, muttering, "I have a boss to report to too."

June laughed and leaned forward. "Oh yeah? Who is that?"

Eris pointed out of the office window then, and June turned, her breath catching in her throat. A cold sinking feeling took over as she watched three men in navy suits walk through the front door.

Terror gripped June. "How much money?"

"A lot."

June nodded. She watched them stop, and the middle suit asked a worker something, to which he responded by pointing to the window that she peered through. She spun and faced Eris. "Why are they here?"

She spoke softly, voice barely above a whisper. "Their boss is my boss, dear. He's the boss of New York."

Understanding dawned on June then. Typhon had been serious when he said that Poseidon was set to take over everything. There was no denying that her fate was now intertwined with his.

"Eris, on the topic of honesty, where can I find him?" She glanced through the window to see the trio getting closer, and her legs shook.

Eris gave another nonchalant shrug. "I'm not sure." June glared at her until she finally rolled her eyes and said, "There's a gentleman's club. Middle of downtown. Try there. I'll see if I can find someone to meet you."

"Thanks," June breathed before standing. She started to move to the door, but Eris stopped her, steely eyes holding June's green ones.

"Understand something. This is way bigger than you. And I hold loyalties to no individual. Next time we meet, I may not be so accommodating. We are all just pawns trying to stay on the board."

June nodded, the hairs on her neck raising. "I wouldn't fault you. You're a god, after all," she said stiffly, and a Cheshire grin stretched across Eris' face.

June went to the door and realized that she couldn't run past the suits without getting caught. Her heart pounded as they were stopped by the man with the papers just twenty feet away.

Eris cleared her throat, and June whirled to see her pointing at a door to the side of the office. June thanked her again and burst through it into the bright sun shining onto a small parking lot. Sunshine after a gray morning had to be a good omen, she thought.

She began running across the parking lot, her oversized boots clumping loudly with each step. Dizziness started to take over her again, and she silently begged it to stop. She couldn't get sick right now. As she threw herself through a thin gap in the fence to the street beyond, a deep voice yelled, "Hey!" from the office door.

Her feet slapped the pavement hard, and she didn't stop running until she heard something behind her. As she turned, her foot caught the curb, and she fell toward the road. Her arms flung out on instinct, but instead of connecting with asphalt, she found herself falling through the stars.

29

Helen's eyes were crusted over, and she rubbed her face into the cloth pulled over them to help ease her eyelids open. A rumble from underneath her muffled the voices that spoke nearby, and as she strained her ears, something bumped her around and her head was whacked against the ceiling. She cracked open one eye, but found that it was just as dark as if she kept them closed, and when she tried to move, a spasm shot up her left shoulder. As she moved to her right, she realized that her hands were bound behind her back. She fought to roll around and kicked her feet out, to no avail. She opened her mouth to scream, but brakes squeaked underneath her and she froze.

A moment later, light flooded through the holes in the bag.

"She's awake," a gruff voice said.

A pair of hands grabbed her arms and lifted her up, but as she stood, her legs gave out, and hands gripped her on either side and guided her over a pitted walkway.

The feeling began to come back into her limbs as she was dragged up a flight of stairs.

"Where are we going?" she asked.

No one answered, and a minute later, the noises around her changed. A few voices spoke from far away, and a shuffling sound filled the air. She was set down in a chair before something was wrapped around her ankles, and her shoulders sagged.

The cloth was finally removed from her face, and she blinked rapidly at how bright the room was. She craned her stiff neck to see a few men sitting at a table, and as she turned, her jaw dropped. She blinked again and heard a chuckle behind her at her shock.

On the other side of the room, what appeared to be a man paced, but instead of a human head, as he should have, his face was contorted into a beak like a hawk, and large wings had torn through his shirt. She tried to move her feet back, but the binding around them tightened. Her gaze dropped, and she nearly screamed at the snake that wound around her feet.

Before she could look too closely at the rest of the room, a man in a pin-striped suit stepped in front of her and leaned down. "It's nice to meet you, Helen."

She looked up and into a pair of deep-blue eyes, and the anxiety in her stomach settled. She tried to open her mouth but found her mind blank.

"I'm glad that you could join me here. Though, I am disappointed that I am unable to find William."

Helen's mouth went dry, and she looked between the man's eyes, trying to think of something to say. A nerve in his forehead twitched, and he straightened, brushing back the gray hair at his temple.

"What do you mean?" she finally asked.

As he stepped away, she took a deep breath, and her chest tightened. She twisted her ankles against their binds, but found no give.

He turned back around. "I *mean* he stole from me and disappeared. He may as well have spat in my face."

"Are you Don?"

"Am I—Of course I am? Are you stupid?" he spat the question at her, and she flinched.

Helen kept her gaze trained on him as she tried to listen to what was happening around the room. He turned and walked toward the window before pacing back toward her.

"I didn't know," she said quietly.

"Well, sometimes what you don't know *will* kill you." His face contorted angrily before he snapped at someone that she couldn't see. "Show her to her room." Don looked back at her. "William can collect you as soon as his debt is paid."

Before Helen could open her mouth to protest, a woman spoke behind her, and her face was covered again.

30

June opened her eyes to find herself in the familiar glistening white marble room, but something was wrong this time.

The massive opening in the ceiling that let in the sun was falling in on itself and the marble columns supporting the walls were crumbling. The sky was no longer bright, but gray and dreary. Lightning arced through the sky, and she turned her head up to look. She dove out of the way as a chunk of gold the size of a car fell where she had just been standing. The sounds around her finally came into focus, and she heard people screaming in an odd language. She grabbed the side of her head to try to stop the ringing in her ears. Her vision was blurred, but she could make out other people in white robes, running this way and that.

She scrambled up quickly, shaking the daze from her head, just as a piece of marble to her right crashed down, shaking the floor and causing a loud cracking sound to echo through the air. June swiveled around and watched as two figures ran through the exit she had visited before, and she took off after them, dodging and weaving as pieces of rock and gold tumbled down around her. Screams filled her ears as she pumped her arms and ran. She dove through the arch as it fell in on itself.

Landing hard on the ground on her stomach, she groaned and pushed herself up, suddenly aware of the fact that the screams had stopped and the world was quiet. She stood and brushed the dirt from her dress. Where was the robe she wore previously in this dream? She looked up to see over twenty people staring at her in mute silence. Some threw their hands up and gasped, and some glared at her with open hatred. She lifted her hand and quietly said, "Hello."

"June?" The voice called her name from somewhere in the crowd. "June!" it exclaimed frantically, and she watched as Typhon pushed forward through the mass of people, splitting the group in two. He ran to her and embraced her, but she was too shocked to move.

"Ty? Why are you here?"

He pulled back, and she got a good look at him. He was Typhon, but also not. His skin had a red glow to it, and he'd sprouted horns. His deep voice was the same, but he was taller than normal and much more muscular as well, and he was wearing a piece of the white cloth that made up most robes, but it was only tied around his waist. June looked away and blushed. "Can you maybe put a shirt on?"

Typhon looked down and said, "Oh!" before waving his hand in front of him in a swirl. Suddenly he stood in front of June in the same way he'd appeared through her childhood—nicely pressed suit, driver's cap, normal human-looking skin, no horns.

June smiled and gave him a proper hug. "What's going on here?"

He shook his head. "It's quite the story. What are *you* doing here?"

She shrugged. "Visiting. This is my dream, after all." Typhon froze and looked at her curiously before glancing behind him and taking her hand to lead her away from the crowd.

The sky was still dreary, but the sounds of crashing and stone had stopped, and she couldn't hear screams anymore as they walked together in the grass. Typhon stopped them among some wildflowers and sat down, and June followed suit.

"June, this isn't a dream. This is Olympus. Who knows how you found it, but you're not meant to be here," Typhon said cautiously.

June's jaw dropped as she looked around. It made sense. This place was gorgeous, unearthly. "But I can't help when I come. I fall asleep or close my eyes and wake up here. Then 'here' crumbles, and I wake up back at home."

Typhon held up his hands. "Hold on, what do you mean it crumbles?"

June explained her last visit, her meeting with the gray-eyed man, and how the ground fell out from under her before she fell through stars.

Typhon's face went white. "June, I don't think you were dreaming. I think you were seeing a prophecy."

June blinked at him, confused.

"It's rare, but sometimes mortals, when exposed to a god at one time or another, develop some sort of power based on their personality. Normally it's small, something like their memory improving, or they are a bit stronger than before. It's possible that since you spent your entire childhood with me, and then were blessed by another god, that something more came out."

June threw up her hands. "Why does this keep happening to me!"

Typhon furrowed his brow. "I think there's someone you need to meet."

June stood and followed as he led her further through the grass. A tall marble wall, maybe to whatever was behind the large room she had appeared in, ran parallel to their right, and a dense forest sat to their left. Wildflowers speckled the grass beneath their feet, and June swore she heard something, or someone, whisper from a tree as she passed close to it. They walked for a few minutes until Typhon stopped. June, who'd been so focused on the grass and flowers at her feet, nearly ran into him. She stepped back and looked up, sucking in a sharp breath.

A large stable, unlike anything she'd ever seen, stood in front of them. It had gilded walls, with mahogany support beams. There were six separate stalls, and a horse twice her height stood in each one. They were bright white, with deep-black eyes and gold-tipped manes. June stepped forward to look closer, and one of the mares snorted. The sound was like a cannon boom, and she guessed, based on its size, that it likely sounded the same when it began running.

She stepped back next to Typhon, who leaned down and whispered, "Apollo's steeds." June nodded, and Typhon cupped his hands around his mouth to yell, "Hey, Apollo!"

A golden head popped up in the second-to-last stall, and June giggled nervously at the start it gave her. The man's hair looked like hand-spun gold, as if something had created thread from sunlight and carefully sewn every strand of hair into his head. He seemed to grow slightly smaller as he approached them, shrinking to Typhon's height as he stopped in front of June and held out his hand, an impish grin on his face.

June blushed and looked down, only to realize that Apollo was completely naked. She looked away as Typhon smacked Apollo's outstretched hand. "Be decent. We need your help."

June watched a flicker of irritation pass over Apollo's face before he spun in a quick circle, rich purple robes appearing as he slowed to a stop.

Even in dark clothing, the god radiated light. His skin glowed, and his teeth sparkled when he grinned. "What can I do for you?" He addressed Typhon but kept eye contact with June. She was sure that her face was still red.

Typhon cleared his throat and motioned away from the stable. "Perhaps where there aren't ears?"

Apollo agreed and led the way to a small bench, where he sat. Typhon and June found a place on the ground, and Apollo's grin widened, as if he was proud of himself for sitting higher than the others.

"This is June, my ward. And I believe she may have an ability that will interest you."

Apollo waved his hand nonchalantly. "Yes, I know all about our new little mortal protector. Likes to cause trouble and kill off men to protect the women, yeah?" He winked at June, and her embarrassment colored her cheeks.

"Yes, well, I believe we also may have a new oracle in the making."

Apollo took on a puzzled look and leaned in toward June, eyeing her up and down. "No. Not possible."

Ty blanched. "What do you mean?"

"All my oracles are already in place, and I have an innate connection to all of them." He wagged his finger at June's stomach. "That one, however, may be a different story. I do sense the power there."

June self-consciously placed a hand over her belly and looked down. She looked back up to find Typhon staring at her, with a question in his eyes.

She nodded slowly. Though she hadn't taken her dream seriously when the man with gray eyes congratulated her, it was the only explanation the hospital had as well.

"So, even though I'm not an oracle, a baby could be giving me visions?"

Apollo jerked his chin down in a nod. "It's not unheard of. Although, it is strange, if you are carrying a human child. You are just mortal, correct?"

Typhon picked at a cuticle, looking uneasy as his eyes widened at her before he looked back at Apollo. "I assume so, but we're not sure. Haven't really had a chance to test it."

Apollo nodded again and clapped his hands before standing. "Well, this has been nice, but I really must be going."

Typhon scrambled to his feet. "Wait! There was a vision. That's why we came."

Apollo lowered himself back to his seat, intrigue clear on his face. "Go on."

June launched into the story of her dream of everything going dark and falling through the ground. Apollo's face paled, his glow dimming for a moment before asking, "And you're sure of this?"

June confirmed, and the god placed his chin in his hand, looking lost in thought.

"Do you know what caused the fall in the main hall today?"

June shook her head. Apollo's face looked grim. "Poseidon has been wreaking havoc on the mortal world of late. Then he brought it here. I believe he has the intention of taking down Olympus, or someone does. Either way, the monsters he stole from Hades were sent here, and there was a bit of a battle before you showed."

"But why? Why go through all this trouble?"

Apollo shrugged. "Boredom, perhaps. Or it's just that he really wants Zeus' position. He's been slighted for too long."

June nodded. "What do we do, then?"

Typhon whispered, "Kill him."

June turned her head quickly and looked at her friend. How did one kill a god?

As if he'd read her mind, Apollo said, "He can only be killed here, but another god can't be the one to do it. If he dies down there, then he'll just come back here. But if someone can force him to come here in his mortal form, and Zeus can neutralize him, then we won't have to worry about it anymore."

June nodded and looked around thoughtfully. "How?"

Apollo shrugged. "If you're able to hop back and forth, maybe you can bring someone with you."

"What if I can't control it?"

Apollo laughed. "You'll have to figure it out." He promptly rose, spun, and disappeared in a flash of light.

Typhon sighed and stood as well, reaching down to help June up. He gave her a quick squeeze and said, "We'll figure it out. I have to help clean up here, but I'll be down soon." June nodded into his chest and closed her eyes. "I'm sorry you have so much to handle," he said.

"Thank you." She sighed and pulled away, and Typhon offered her a small smile before he pushed her back with a breeze.

31

A tap sounded on the front door moments after June materialized in her living room, and she stumbled toward it. She shoved windswept hair away from her face and swung the door open.

"What?" she asked before realizing who waited on the other side. "Oh, hi. What are you doing here?"

Henry froze and looked at her, seeming confused. "I thought you would want a friend after the trip." He twisted his fingers together and looked at the ground. "Plus I thought continuing to be here might make up for the miscommunication."

She took a deep breath, wringing her hands and moving back to let him in. It felt as if an entire week had passed since he'd dropped off the jumpsuit, but a glance at the clock showed it had only been a few hours.

He busied himself making tea while she leaned back in the chair and kicked off the ridiculous boots.

Henry handed her a hot cup, and she took it gratefully while he slid into the seat across from her. Her mind raced, trying to think of how she was going to let Henry in on what was going on.

He looked at her as the silence stretched between them. She finally blurted out, "Eris was his boss," before taking a long draw from her mug. Henry's jaw dropped, and June nodded at his shocked expression. "And Don is her boss."

"Eris?" he asked.

June nodded.

Henry carefully set down his cup with shaking hands. "My Don?"

"Our Don," she corrected.

"That's who sent me to ask questions, you know."

June groaned. "I knew, but it didn't click. He's the reason I—" She stopped herself. "Never mind."

Henry gave her a sad look. "We will figure this out together."

"We? This is on me, Henry. My mother was the one taken. My father was the one who put us in debt."

"I can help!" he exclaimed. "We'll figure it out together."

June leaned in, raising an eyebrow at him. "Why do you want to help, Henry? What do you have to gain aside from information to feed back to Don?"

Henry shook his head. "I'm not going to tell him anything, at least nothing like this. You're just trying to figure out what's been hidden from you to better pay back the debt. The extent of my job regarding you was to get answers about William's whereabouts." He leaned forward, his fingers brushing against her knuckles. "And, frankly, I like you."

June smiled. "If you want to help, there are some things you need to know. And"—she raised a finger—"you can't just bust into ladies' homes anymore."

Henry grinned sheepishly and nodded.

As if on cue, a gust of wind blew the window open. Three stray leaves landed on the kitchen floor, and June clasped her hands, looking at Henry intently.

"Henry, what do you know about the gods?"

He looked a bit shaken. "I'm not sure. I guess I never really believed they existed."

June breathed deeply before speaking, worried he might think she was crazy and get up and run away. "We don't have the luxury of time to ease you in—what if I told you that there was more to the world than you could believe?"

Henry gripped his cup tightly enough to turn his knuckles white. "I'm not sure." He seemed anxious, and June smiled to reassure him.

"The gods walk among us, Henry," she said, before turning to face the empty kitchen. "Alright, Ty," she announced.

Henry blinked at her, and then suddenly the breeze swirled again and Typhon stood where the leaves were before. His tan suit was crisp and new-looking, and he'd changed out the brown driver's cap for a tweed one. Henry jumped back in his chair, and she tried not to smile. Typhon inclined his head, walking up with his hand outstretched to shake Henry's.

Henry took it, a look of awe and confusion on his face. "H-hi," he stuttered.

Typhon gripped his hand firmly and said hello before taking a seat between June and Henry.

June cleared her throat. "This is Typhon, Titan God of Wind and Storm . . ." She looked to Ty for confirmation, and he nodded.

Henry's voice shook as he spoke. "It's nice to meet you."

Typhon laughed lightly. "It's okay, I'm not going to smite you. And you can call me Ty. This one has her whole life." He jerked a thumb at June, and she laughed lightly.

Blush creeped in Henry's cheeks, and he nodded, as if he was scared to say anything else. June reached across the table and took his hand.

"There's more. Don is actually Poseidon. Typhon could explain it better, but essentially he came down here to wreak havoc and became the 'boss of New York,' as Eris put it." Henry swallowed hard, but she continued. "When he attacked me in that alley, Athena came after and gave me a blessing. Those statues of men downstairs? I created them. When I look a man in the eye, I can turn him to stone."

Henry jumped up. "You mean to tell me that you could have killed me at any point?"

June smiled sheepishly. "I suppose." She quickly stood as well and held her hands out. "But I didn't, and I don't think I will. I've started getting a handle on it, and I feel safe with you."

Henry ran a hand through his hair and looked around the room as if he was trying to look anywhere but her eyes. June and Typhon exchanged a look but stayed quiet.

After a few minutes of pacing, Henry fell back in his chair, laughing in disbelief. "Remind me never to make you mad."

June laughed, and Typhon cleared his throat to bring her back on track.

"Is that why you wear the sunglasses?" Henry asked, words coming slowly.

June nodded. "It helps to have a physical barrier so no accidents happen."

She reached across the table to give Henry's hand a squeeze, and he returned the gesture, still looking uneasy, before she continued. "Back to the point. Don is a dangerous man, and he needs to be dealt with. I'm sure of the fact that he took my mother now, but I've no idea where to find him. I need to find her and pay him off to get her back."

Henry groaned. "How on earth did you ever get involved with him?"

"I didn't!" she exclaimed. "My father did. I know he had a gambling issue, and Eris said he was in debt at work. I'm sure this is all coincidence at this point, but Poseidon is owed big time, and he's trying to collect any way he can. Eris wouldn't tell me how much my father owed, but she said Don visits a club near downtown."

Henry cocked his head. "Spades, maybe?"

June blushed at the idea of Henry visiting a club like that and took a moment to recover. "That's what I thought, but I'm sure that closed when I was a child."

Henry shrugged, and Typhon chimed in. "You know not everything is as it seems, especially since the prohibition. A lot of, ah, Olympians and such have opened clubs underground." He shrugged. "It may be worth a shot." He glanced at his watch. "Sorry, kids," he said, standing. "I've got a date with a storm." He winked at June and in a second was gone, twisting on a breeze out the window.

Henry's jaw dropped as he stared after the leaves disappearing in the distance. "Does he do that all the time?"

June laughed at that, a full happy sound, and shook her head. "You'll get used to it."

Henry nodded, roughly scrubbing his hands over his face. "I'm not sure it will ever sink in so that I can." He stood and checked his watch. "It's already nearly seven!" He put his hands flat on the table, leaning forward with a mischievous twinkle in his eye. "Miss Juniper Georgian, may I take you to dinner?"

June shook her head, not thinking he was serious. He held his gaze on her, and her smile faltered.

Butterflies surged up in her stomach, and she fiddled with her watch. "I've never been on a real date, Henry. Plus, I feel like I shouldn't be relaxing with my mom gone."

Henry reached across the table and took her hand, wrapping his fingers in hers. "Then, let me be the first. I promise it will be fun, and it's healthy to take a break. I need to take my mind off of all of this." She finally nodded, and Henry smiled. "Go get ready. We'll leave soon."

June gave his fingers a squeeze and went upstairs.

Getting ready for a real date was stress-inducing, to put it lightly. She couldn't think of a single thing to wear, and she finally opted for a simple light-pink dress that fell below her knees and a dark-blue coat that matched his.

She returned downstairs after almost half an hour and was greeted by Henry, who was standing awkwardly at the bottom step holding a bouquet of flowers. She smiled and took them graciously, hurrying to find a vase before taking his hand and leaving home.

Henry ran ahead of her to open the passenger side of his car and held out a hand to help her in. They drove in awkward silence until June finally spoke up as they passed Wall Street. "Where are we going?"

Henry smiled. "It's a surprise." He pulled the car up on the side of the road and moved quickly to help June out, making sure she didn't land too hard on her feet. He held out his arm, and she wrapped her small hand around it, before they fell into step together and ventured down the block. When they approached a corner, June gasped. A tall, gorgeous building stood in front of them. With carved moldings on the outside, the building stood at least six stories high that she could see. She recognized the entrance as Delmonico's, one of the nicest restaurants in the city.

"No, we can't!" she exclaimed, turning to Henry, who gave her a goofy grin.

"We can and will."

They walked through the open door together, still arm in arm, and met a server who took them to a beautifully set table near the back. After they were seated, June leaned in to whisper, "This is so nice!"

Henry laughed and looked over his menu. June set hers down and said, "I can't decide. Will you?"

He nodded, and when the server returned, Henry wrote the order down, careful not to show June. She laughed at him.

When they were alone again, she wasn't sure how to break the silence, so she simply held Henry's hand across the table. He looked at her intently, studying her face, and warmth crept into her cheeks. "You have the most gorgeous eyes, Miss Georgian. Like new flower buds waiting to bloom."

She blushed a deep shade of crimson, stuttering out a thank you.

When the server returned, she was shocked by the large plate set in front of her. Piled with a glistening piece of steak and a helping of mashed carrots, a dish with caviar, and a platter of breads and oils, she threw her hands up to cover her mouth and gasped. "This is too much!"

Henry smiled. "Nothing is too much for you."

June beamed and dug into her dinner.

After a long few minutes of eating, Henry cleared his throat. "So, what's the plan now?"

June set her fork down and gave him a sad look, as the magic of the night dissipated and everything came back. Her mother was missing, her family owed a massive debt, and she was pregnant with the child of a god. What was she supposed to do? She sighed. "I'm not sure. I think I need to go to Spades. Eris mentioned sending someone."

Henry nodded. "Shall I come with?"

"I appreciate your help, but no. I need to do this alone. If he's there, I don't want you to see what might happen." She didn't mention the fact that she didn't fully trust him, and she didn't want to end up with a Henry-sized statue in her gallery if her power went haywire. Gods knew what might happen if someone she liked got involved in a sticky situation.

"This has all been a lot to take in, but I think I sort of always had a feeling." Henry waved his fork a bit. "You know, I was never religious, but my mother regularly prayed to Aphrodite. She would take every chance to keep her marriage to my father strong."

June laughed and nodded. "Yeah, my parents weren't religious at all. Mom tried to educate me on the other Pantheons to keep me unbiased, but I think since Typhon came around, we all had a feeling. At one point my father tried to suggest that maybe there was only one god!" Henry laughed, and June smirked. "Imagine, one god doing all that work. Especially now that I know what Typhon does, I couldn't picture him handling everything in this realm."

"I'm glad I know, I think. I almost feel more secure. I wonder if they answer our prayers, though."

June looked away thoughtfully, remembering the night that she had thought of Athena and received her blessing. "I think they do to an extent. Athena came to my aid, in her own strange way."

They finished their meal quietly, and as Henry was about to help June from her seat, she suddenly felt sick. "I'm sorry, I'll be right back."

She dashed past the tables next to them and rounded a corner, stopping as someone tall and broad blocked her path. She stumbled back, keeping her gaze to the floor so as not to hurt an innocent person, and apologized. The familiar smell hit her as the voice reached her ears.

"Well, hello, June." Don's gravel-coated words sent a shock up her spine, and she looked up to meet his eyes.

Anger crashed over her, and she balled her fists, ready to swing as she looked at him. A second passed. Then another. She looked down at his feet, shocked to see that they were still completely normal with no sign of stone.

She looked back up and whispered, "Poseidon."

He grinned at her, almost baring his teeth as he leaned down and whispered in her ear, "Did you pass on my message?"

She tried to shove him back but was instead forced to step back herself. She glared up at him. "What did you do with my mother?" she demanded.

He chuckled and stepped closer. "Don't worry, she's well taken care of. I wouldn't dare hurt her." The color drained in June's face, and she tried to stutter out an accusation, but her words failed her. He grabbed her raised hands in his, shoving her against a wall. "Are you here to pay more of your father's debt? You know, he owes me a lot."

She squirmed between him and the solid brick she was pinned against and opened her mouth to scream, but he raised a finger.

"Uh-uh. Can't have that." He leaned down until his face was barely an inch from hers. "Have you moved on from me already, June?" He nodded toward the main dining area of the restaurant. "I see you've seduced one of my employees."

June was suddenly filled with strength from her anger, and she shoved him back. "I haven't seduced anyone, and you were never an interest of mine!" She shoved him back again. "Tell me where my mother is!" she yelled. She wanted to yank his silver tie down and wrap it around his throat. As if he read her mind, he straightened it and pulled the hem of his jacket down.

"I'm keeping her somewhere William will know to look." June stepped forward, intent on shoving him again, and a wave of nausea suddenly came over her. She froze in her tracks, looked at the ground, and vomited on Don's black loafers. Behind her, Henry skidded to a stop at the end of the hall, and Poseidon's eyes flicked to him for a moment before turning back on June. Fear settled in as she realized what she'd done. He opened his mouth, then closed it. She could feel rage emanating off him.

He finally set a smile on his face, clearly devoid of joy, and raised his foot from the puddle covering it. "Weak girl," he spat.

Poseidon pulled his jacket down and straightened his tie again. As he shoved past Henry, he stopped to declare, "You're fired, obviously." The squelch from his shoes echoed through the restaurant as he walked out. June sank to the ground, and

Henry fell next to her in time to slide his arm around her shoulders. They sat together for a few minutes until a server came and shooed them out.

Henry held June by the arm until they were outside, where she turned and fell into his chest. Tears started sliding down her face, and he gripped her tightly.

"What am I supposed to do?" she whispered.

The corner of his mouth tugged up. "You mean 'we'? I just lost my job, you know."

June frowned at that and pulled back to look at him. Her eyes glistened in the dim light, and his face was riddled with concern. He leaned down, barely an inch away from her, and she stood as tall as she could to close the gap between them. His eyes widened as her lips touched his, and butterflies overtook her stomach. His eyes slid shut, and he squeezed her tighter until she finally pulled back, breathing in sharply.

Blush bloomed on her cheeks, and he clasped her hand and began to walk toward her apartment, both of them still laughing.

"I'm sorry my life is so crazy. And I'm sorry you're wrapped up in this nonsense," June said.

Henry pulled her to a stop and placed both hands on her face. "Hey, I wouldn't be here if I didn't want to be."

She nodded, and he brushed his lips against hers again before they continued walking.

They both stopped in front of June's door, and Henry let go of her hand. He ran a hand through his hair and looked around. "I guess—"

June cut him off. "Would you like to come up?"

"I'd like that. I'll have to go fetch my car later."

June looked around, just realizing that they'd walked all the way home, and they laughed together again as she opened the door. This was the lightest she had felt in ages, despite the run-in with Poseidon.

She led the way to the kitchen and stopped in her tracks in the doorway, narrowing her eyes at the dining table.

Henry stepped up behind her and asked, "What's wrong?"

"Asclepius," she muttered.

He stumbled back, and pointed, voice laced with fear. "That's the snake that follows you!"

June turned back to face the snake and crossed her arms. "What do you want, Pius?"

The god writhed up from their scales, and Henry let out a high-pitched squeak, which June ignored. Seconds later, where a large black reptile had been now sat Asclepius. They looked different than normal, with their gold makeup faded and normally slick hair mussed. June continued to stare, and the god finally broke the silence.

"That's a hell of a greeting for an old friend."

"This is Asclepius, god of being a nuisance."

Asclepius looked ruffled at the insult but stuck their tongue in their cheek without saying anything. Henry stepped forward, raised his hand, then immediately dropped it and looked at June in bewilderment.

He stepped closer to the god and said, "I'm sorry, sir, I'm just not quite sure how to meet your . . . ah, type, yet." His voice trailed off, and Asclepius laughed, hopping down from their seat on the edge of the table to stand.

They towered over Henry. "Well, first off, I'm not a sir. You can call me Asclepius, or"—they shot a dirty look at June—"Pius, as this one does. And second, traditionally anything from offerings of small animals to a bowing worship would be accepted. But I suppose we are in more modern times now, so a cup of tea will do."

Henry inclined his head awkwardly and moved to put the kettle on, busying himself by pulling mugs and silk tea pouches from the cabinet while Asclepius sat down. June slid into the chair opposite them and glared at them as they propped their elbows on the table and rested their chin on their hands.

"What do you want?" she asked, trying to keep the accusation from her voice. She was not happy with their last interaction and certainly wasn't going to let them off easily.

"Oh, nothing, just checking in to see what's happening."

June rolled her eyes. "Cut it, Pius. I'm tired of all you gods playing games with me. I'm not in the mood."

Asclepius sighed. "I'm serious, I'm just here to check in."

She eyed them suspiciously before saying, "I'm going to a gentleman's club."

Henry set a mug of tea in front of both of them. Pius picked it up, raised an eyebrow at June, and asked, "Oh?"

June nodded firmly. "Apparently Poseidon frequents the place, so I'll be going to try and find out where my mother is."

Asclepius laughed. "Brilliant! Because nothing could go wrong with a slight woman barely over five feet facing the God of the Sea himself!"

June glared at them until they stopped laughing at their own comment. "I'll have you know that I saw him today, actually, and came out in one piece."

Asclepius gave her an incredulous look. "And you're still looking for him? Didn't you turn him?"

June shook her head sadly. "I tried, but it didn't work . . . maybe I used it all up?"

Asclepius shrugged, then suddenly cocked their head, as if they'd heard someone yell their name. They began to morph down into a pile of scales, hissing, "Good luck," as they went.

Shock and confusion bled into her. "Pius?" she whispered. Then he was gone.

Henry finally walked back over from his spot by the sink and looked at the seat Asclepius had been sitting in, examining it as if the god might suddenly pop back up.

"Um, where did"—he hesitated—"they go?"

June shook her head. "I don't know."

Henry looked at the clock and moved to June, crouching in front of her. "I should go, but I'll come by tomorrow before you go to the club. Will you be okay?"

She nodded and gave him a peck on the cheek. "Thank you for tonight."

He smiled. "Of course."

Then June was alone. She looked at the table, where she had abandoned a stack of mail the night before, and lifted the letter from the doctor. Tears pricked her eyes as she placed a hand on her stomach. Though the doctor and Zeus confirmed her pregnancy, her belly was still flat and felt quite normal.

"Are you in there?" she asked. Of course, nothing happened.

32

Typhon drifted over a large gate, spikes breaking his breeze as he avoided the fence. He shook his head as he looked at the massive manor in front of him. It looked almost like a warehouse from the outside—a massive iron box with black windows. As he rounded the front, the door swung wide open. He took himself down and landed on the front step, straightening his jacket as he stepped in. A small, balding man stood with his hand on the lever, bowing slightly.

"Good evening, Last Titan. Mistress Eris is in the lounge."

Typhon nodded firmly and headed to the right, but the old man cleared his throat. Typhon turned to see him pointing to a nearly closed door in the opposite direction, and his lip twitched as he walked that way.

He approached the door and froze in his tracks before he made it through the frame.

Eris was in the room, indeed. She was perched on the back of a couch facing a large fireplace. With a black silk robe falling from her shoulder and barely covering her waist, Typhon could clearly see the outline of her breasts against the firelight. He took a step back as she threw her head back and moaned loudly.

As Typhon was about to turn, he caught sight of a head bobbing between her legs, her feet resting on the poor bastard's shoulders. She gripped the edge of the couch and the man reached out and pulled himself further into her. Typhon shook his head and summoned a breeze to shoot through the house, ignoring the moans that filled the air behind him.

As he explored and tried to shake the image of what he'd walked in on, he realized that *house* was an understatement. In his personally guided tour, he found sixteen bedrooms, nine bathrooms, a piano room, and a restaurant-sized kitchen—not to mention the entire lower level of staff accommodations.

He finally stopped in the foyer again, nearly tripping over one of his leaves while he tried not to bang into a massive sculpture. He straightened and pulled his jacket down, and when he looked up, Eris was standing in front of him with her arms crossed and a grim look on her face. At least she had tied her robe up.

"Spying, are we?" She raised an eyebrow at him.

"Just killing time while you finished molesting that poor mortal."

Eris laughed, and the sharp sound echoed around them. "It's not molesting if they come to me."

Her eyes twinkled as she turned back to the lounge and motioned for Typhon to follow. He felt a bit green as he thought about that. If any of the gods were to be given the title *of the whores*, it should be Eris.

They settled into couches opposite each other, and Eris crossed her legs and clasped her hands on top of her knee before leaning forward, an expectant look on her face.

Typhon cleared his throat, trying not to think of what had been done on these couches. "I've come to seek an alliance."

Eris cocked her head, frowning for a moment before bursting into laughter. Typhon's jaw twitched, and her laugh faded as she regarded his tense expression. Her eyes widened. "You can't be serious?"

He motioned around. "You've been here for a hundred years. Don't you think it's time to actually help somewhere?"

Eris jumped up, and her robe fell open from the motion. Typhon flinched as she yelled, "I do help! I help Poseidon every *fucking* day."

Typhon sighed and motioned for her to sit back down, which she did with a huff.

"I know you've been on his side in the past, but you can't possibly believe in him anymore. He's the reason for June's situation, and in turn, responsible for the demise of someone you were close with, correct?"

Blush rose into her cheeks as she swore, then waved her hand. "That was just a minor casualty. No one important."

Typhon smirked. "Oh, you just lured an innocent to the park for a quickie that was interrupted?"

"Exactly. It's not my problem if she mistook role-playing for something else."

Typhon leaned back and crossed his arms. "You're really happy being on his side?"

Eris' face fell as she picked a nail, eyes trained down. "I don't have a choice."

"What do you mean? Look around! You've managed a building plant for years, swept hundreds of men off their feet, and managed to secure this mansion. You've become just as important as him here."

She looked up sadly. "I'm just a prisoner in this war, Ty. Head of recruitment because he forces me to be, and living in a pretty cage."

Understanding dawned on him then. "This isn't your place, is it?"

She shook her head.

"Fight back, then!"

She met his gaze, and her throat bobbed. "I've tried." She stood slowly, holding eye contact with Typhon before whispering, "It's not easy to leave." Then, with a loud cracking sound, she blinked out of existence.

He pinched the bridge of his nose before allowing the wind to shuffle around his feet. This was going to be a lot harder than he thought.

33

June stood in the middle of a field. The grasses and golden flowers around reached her knees, and a small creek bubbled nearby.

She looked up to find two moons hanging in the cloudless, dark night, and as she strained her ears, she realized that the air was lacking the sounds of the city or insects she was used to.

"Hello?" she called.

No one answered, and she began walking toward the specks that she knew were the golden gates beyond the bridge.

When she reached the edge of the glade, she caught a glimpse of Typhon in the distance. He waved his arm wildly and jogged over.

"Juniper! How did you get here this time?"

She shrugged and looked around. "I really wish I had an answer for you."

Typhon looked up and past her, and she followed his gaze to the sky, which seemed emptier than the one she was used to.

"I wonder if Hestia knows you're coming here. She set alarms so that Olympians can only arrive and depart to Olympus through the rift."

As June opened her mouth to ask what he meant, he pointed up, and she gasped. Above them, the sky looked as if someone had torn a hole in it; jagged edges opened a seam that winked in and out of visibility and rippled with light from within.

"What is that?"

"It's how we move between the realms. If you can shift into that space between, you can travel anywhere."

She nodded. "I fall through stars that look similar to what is in there—or out of here—but it's also different. Darker, like a pot of ink."

Typhon scrubbed his beard and raised a brow. "I can only think of one place that looks like that."

They turned together and, as if they weighed nothing more than a leaf, caught a breeze that pulled them up. They moved quickly, climbing higher and higher in the sky. Once the buildings beneath them looked like specks, their breeze suddenly expanded, then pulled together quickly, snapping on itself like a rubber band.

When June looked down again, they were above the city. As they drifted down, she caught a glimpse of the marble building from above, and her breath hitched. It was massive. Gold ceilings stretched for miles in every direction. Large openings revealed smaller buildings inside the enclosed city. Typhon took them down into the main hall, and they materialized in the middle of the room. It had been fixed quickly, and nicely. It looked brand new. June landed on her feet and looked around, surprised to see that no one was in the room. Typhon took off toward a hall, and June had to jog to catch up.

"Where is everyone?" she asked.

Typhon shrugged. "Probably in their rooms. It's pretty late here. We work on a different time wave than mortals."

June nodded and continued following him.

They walked down a grand hall, also marble with gold patterns above them. The hall broke into a massive cathedral-style room with multiple paths, and Typhon chose one of the three to their left. They continued weaving like that, and at the third intersection of entries, the floor began sloping down. June was confused but said nothing as they descended. The marble walls began to get darker, and once they started down a steep decline, the walls turned to gray slate. Typhon reached back and took June's hand, pushing forward into the darkness.

"While Olympus is all good things, the void is where criminals are sent. Some of the original titans were shoved in there." He swallowed hard. "Thankfully Zeus needed me for something, so I stayed. But once you go in, you do not come out."

"How do you get there?" June chewed her bottom lip.

Typhon shook his head. "It's hard to explain. We call it a void, but it's more like a vortex." He reached out a hand, and she took it. "I'll show you."

After nearly twenty minutes of walking, June was out of breath and had a stitch in her side. Finally, Typhon took one last turn to the right, and they stopped at the end of a short hallway. It was dark, with only a small bit of light coming from a sconce on the wall. A dark obsidian door stood in front of them, barely large enough for one person to squeeze through.

Typhon turned to June. "Whatever you do, do not touch it. Don't look too far into it either. It's easy to succumb to its call."

June's hands trembled and her stomach flipped as Typhon reached in front of her and swung the door open wide. Inside were walls of black, and a large ball floated a few feet from June. It had the same look as the star-spotted darkness that June fell through in her dreams. She was urged to reach out and touch it.

She took a step forward, and a silky voice caressed her mind.

Hello, child. You've come to meet me in person this time.

She stumbled backward and stared into the center of the void as it spoke.

What help have you come to seek? Or have you instead come to take a step into the unknown?

June reached a hand toward the ball, and a shiver went down her spine. A spark of light emitted from the orb and raced up her finger, disappearing on the back of her hand.

"What are you?" she asked, voice barely above a whisper.

I have many names. But I prefer Chaos.

June nodded before swallowing hard. "I think I'm looking for a way to get rid of Poseidon."

Heavy silence filled the room as the darkness throbbed and grew around her. Finally, the voice slid across the back of her mind again.

I can take him. Bring him to me and he will be with the rest.

"Rest? Rest of what?" Her voice seemed to meld with the black tendrils that had begun to wrap around her body. She was Chaos. Chaos was her. The stars grew brighter.

The rest of the . . . disposed.

Before June could respond, a hand yanked her back, and she gasped for air as the room spun around her. Typhon turned her around and inspected her. "What were you doing?" he demanded.

June exhaled, the spinning in her head beginning to slow. "I was talking with it. Didn't you hear?"

Typhon shook his head, concern obvious. "You didn't say anything. You just kept shuffling closer and closer."

June looked down and studied her hands. "I-I don't understand."

Typhon grabbed her arm and pulled her away from the door, out into the hallway. She leaned against the cold marble, enjoying the sensation on the back of her neck, and slid to the floor.

"Chaos said it'll take Poseidon. I just have to bring him." She looked up at Typhon, anxious. "But how?"

Typhon crouched in front of her, brow furrowed. "It is Chaos?" He rubbed the spot between his eyebrows and pinched the bridge of his nose. "Never mind. You need to learn to shift. Clearly you did it in your dreams, but we need to figure out how to do it for real." He held out a hand, which June accepted, and he pulled her to stand and walk with him. "What exactly did it say?"

"Bring Poseidon, and Chaos will take him. It also . . . knew me. It said I came to meet in person this time."

Typhon nodded. "So your dreams have been real."

June stopped and turned to face him. "I've been through Chaos before. I fell through it both times that I left Olympus. I fell straight through and then back home."

Typhon's brow furrowed. "I'm not sure what that means."

"It also said that Poseidon would be with the rest—with the disposed."

Typhon's spine stiffened, and his walk slowed. "The other titans. We didn't know where they actually *went* after going into the void." He turned to her with a serious look on his face. "Did it tell you?"

She shook her head. "No, just that he would be with them."

Typhon resumed the climb from the lower level of the void, June on his heels. "But that he would *be*. Which tells me that they still exist . . ." He trailed off and went silent for the rest of the walk. June followed, lost in her own thoughts about jumping from Earth to here.

They wove through the maze of Olympus together until Typhon stopped in front of a gilded door. He reached out a hand and pressed it to the engraved surface, and it melted away at his touch. June's jaw dropped in shock as she followed him in.

A sitting room greeted them, decorated in shades of tan and orange. It looked as if the season of autumn had exploded over the walls and furniture. June stopped in the middle of the room, and Typhon kept going, walking through an arch near the back of the room. He returned after a few seconds holding two large mugs with steam rising from them.

He motioned to one of the couches, and June perched on the edge of it, still gawking. He chuckled and handed her a mug, which she accepted gratefully. The smell of pumpkin and chocolate rose with the steam, and her mouth began watering.

"What is this?"

Typhon raised his glass and took a drink before answering. "My favorite drink."

June smiled. "I meant this place. Where are we?"

Typhon set the cup down and spread his arms wide. "My apologies. Welcome to my home. Or what is my home when I'm in Olympus."

"Wow," was all June could say. She raised the cup to her lips, and warmth filled her as she drank. It was the best thing she had ever tasted. Pumpkin, cinnamon, and chocolate somehow intertwined perfectly and danced across her tongue. A hint of richer spices and black tea followed the symphony, and she closed her eyes and moaned out loud. "This is so good!"

Typhon laughed and winked at her. "There are some perks to being able to come here." He cleared his throat. "Speaking of which—I think we should start by trying to travel between rooms first."

June blanched at him. "Just like that?"

Typhon nodded firmly. "There's not a second to waste. We get an advantage with time passing faster here than in the mortal realm, but if you're to face Poseidon and get rid of him soon, we need to get to work."

June nodded and set her mug down, and the pair rose together.

"Now, we aren't sure if it's your ability or the baby's, so this may take some trial and error. I want you to envision yourself leaving this spot and appearing there." He pointed to the arch behind him. "Shifting is what us gods do to hop around. You've seen me do it plenty, when I ride the wind. Asclepius has too—theirs is collapsing into scales. It varies between us. Apollo disappears into a blink of bright light and essentially travels through beams of sun."

She nodded and closed her eyes, picturing herself zooming over to the arch and opening her eyes to see the living room from the five feet away that it was. She repeated the image on loop, bracing herself and clenching every part of her body possible. Typhon said something, but she ignored it and focused on moving. She felt her body shake a bit, and her eyes snapped open from excitement.

She was still in the same spot. Her face fell, and Typhon offered her a reassuring smile.

"It's okay, you normally do this in your sleep, so it'll be a lot harder now."

June nodded and tried again. This time, sweat beaded on her forehead.

Hours passed like that, with June closing her eyes and straining to move herself with her mind, and Typhon encouraging her every time she opened them again. Finally, she sighed. Her face and neck were hot, and her legs felt weak. She collapsed onto the couch.

"It's no use, Ty. I can't do it."

Typhon moved to crouch next to her. "It's okay, you will get there, I promise." He looked up and noticed the opening in his ceiling was dark. "Let's eat something and try a different method."

June nodded in agreement. After dinner, they practiced until Apollo began to lift the sun. June's entire body was slick with sweat, and Typhon looked exhausted. They had tried everything from forcing the shift to meditating to June hovering on the edge of sleep and imagining moving. Nothing worked. At one point they thought that she may have shifted a couple of inches, but June was sure she'd simply taken a small step by accident.

As they lounged on the couch together, June's head in Typhon's lap and him dozing against the wall, a sudden loud bang shook the house. June jolted, sitting upright and grabbing Typhon's hand. They looked around together. Silence filled the room until a large black cloud drifted over the hole in the ceiling. It looked menacing, with lightning arcing through it and lighting up various spots with blues and purples. June looked up in awe, and Typhon set his mouth in a grimace. He opened it to speak, and a booming voice filled the air around them, cutting him off.

"PO-SEI-DON! HOW DARE YOU!" The voice shook June to her core. She gripped Typhon's hand and blinked, trying to swallow the fear. When she opened her eyes again, they were outside. Typhon and June stared at each other in shock.

"Did you . . .?" she asked.

He shook his head. The boom sounded again, and June ducked involuntarily.

She looked up, and the blood drained from her face. Above them stood a hundred-foot Zeus. He moved slowly but looked terrify-ing nonetheless. Clouds floated around his head, arced with lightning, and she realized that the boom was the thunder emanating from his steps. His skin was purple, with lightning bolts flashing through his veins. He looked down, and she nearly fainted when she saw his face. Where wrinkles were pre-viously, hot electricity outlined his eyes. His beard glowed, and his eyes were white. If Chaos' star-filled blackness was turned in-side out, it would have been Zeus' eyes.

He turned back ahead and took another step past Olympus. June followed his path with her gaze and finally saw what was happening.

Hundreds of bright-red creatures were flying toward them. With four unsettling eyes, feathered skin in shades of red and pink, and strong large wings sprouted from their muscular shoulder blades, they looked terrifying.

She pointed and yelled over the loud crackling coming from Zeus. "What are they?"

"They used to run wild, before Poseidon's minions stole them. They once were gryphons. Poseidon has had someone change them into absolutely terrible things."

June nodded and turned back to the scene. Zeus raised a hand, and lightning shot from his fingertips, blowing down at least twenty of the red creatures. Typhon took her hand and began pulling her away.

"Come on, we shouldn't be here for this. You're not safe."

June pulled her hand back. "But I want to help!"

Typhon turned on her. "You can't help, June! You have a mission. You're not risking your life for Olympus when we won't have anything left if you don't get rid of Poseidon!"

June stepped back, a horrified look on her face. "Why is it up to me to get rid of him? It's your fight! I should get to choose where to participate. I can't even shift, which is the one thing I have to do to beat him. Why don't you do it?"

Typhon sighed and crossed his arms. "You *can* shift! You just did. And there are rules in place for us. We aren't allowed."

June's face heated. "You're all just cowards!"

As if Zeus was cheering for her, another boom clapped through the air around them as she yelled. She turned toward the fight, but mid-spin, she blinked.

When she opened her eyes, the air was still, and she was looking at the obsidian door that led to Chaos. She grumbled and looked around. Unsure if Typhon sent her here or if she brought herself, she stepped up and swung the door open wide. Why here of all places? It was good practice for Poseidon, but was there a point if she couldn't control it? Chaos greeted her with silence. Anger filled her then, followed by discomfort, anxiety, and sadness, each in its own wave. She'd just yelled at her only friend, as she was unsure if Henry truly stood with her or not.

Yes, you have a habit of making trouble out of nothing.

She stepped forward.

It's okay, young one, I have a resting place for you.

Black tentacles caressed her, and she stepped forward once more, falling face-first into the starlight-speckled space.

She felt weightless. Her arms and legs were gone, and she had no heartbeat pounding in her chest. She simply was, and wasn't, at the same time.

Where am I? Her thought left her in a small crumble of light and whizzed around until it sputtered out and faded.

Chaos. The answer wasn't so much spoken as whispered into the very essence of the liquid night that encased her consciousness.

How did I get here? Her words once again balled into a speck of starlight and zigzagged around for a moment.

You walked. The words caressed June, and her essence warmed with the feeling of amusement around her.

Why am I here?

Silence followed her question, and the stars began to blink out of existence one by one.

June began falling then. Down into a pit of blackness, she fell for hours. Or maybe it was seconds. Finally, the rush of air around her stopped, and she floated around a large metal cage. Inside were terrifying-looking creatures. Some had fifty heads and even more arms, some had multiple eyes, and all were massive, sweat-covered, and muscled.

Who— June's question was cut off by a hiss from Chaos.

Disposed.

June stayed silent and watched as the beings ambled about their small space. This would be Poseidon's fate, then.

She forced herself to look away, unsure how it was possible when she couldn't feel her body. How was she meant to learn how to shift, get Poseidon here, and not get sucked in?

Chaos enveloped her once more, and it felt almost as if it were laughing with its entire essence. *You use your fear, child.*

What? What does that mean? Being afraid will help? Stars swirled around her in acknowledgment, but no more words came.

A moment later, the light around her shifted, and began to spin until she was falling, again.

June opened her eyes in the dark, blinking to try and see. Normally those dreams lasted until early morning, but she felt like she was in bed now. This bed felt different, though. It was hard, and her blanket was gone. She heard a sound a few feet away, and her head swiveled of its own accord. A slit of light appeared, casting a dim glow on the room.

It was not her own room. It was small, and the walls were unfinished, with rough concrete slapped here and there. The floor was bare. She looked down at her bed and was shocked to see that it was just a thin mattress on the floor. The door opened wider, and her mouth and body moved on their own again.

She sat up in the bed and with a hoarse voice asked, "Are you going to let me go now?"

June's breath caught. It wasn't her own voice that cracked across the room, it was her mother's. The person on the other side of the door stepped in, and shock shivered up her spine. She tried to gasp and throw her hand to her mouth, but her body wouldn't move. Asclepius stood there, holding a plate with dry food on it.

They appeared more beaten down than before. The last of their golden glow was gone, and their shoulders were slumped. Bruises took up half their face, and when they shuffled into the room, they seemed to have a limp. Asclepius set the plate down at the end of the bed and began to slowly shuffle out. As they reached the door, they stopped for a minute, as if they thought of offering some kind words.

"Let me go home! Please, Denny"

Helen's voice made Asclepius flinch, and they turned and looked at her sadly. "I'm sorry. I have orders."

Suddenly June was flung from her mother's body.

June slammed back into her own bed, gasping for air. She sat up and looked down at her stomach, shaking. Her fingers trembled as she laid her hand there.

She breathed heavily. "What was that?"

<h1 style="text-align:center">34</h1>

The bed that Helen was tied to was as hard as rocks, and she swore every time she tried to shift her weight. She was too damn old for this nonsense. She rolled her hips side to side to try and relieve the pain in them. As she stretched back, a sliver of light popped into existence across the room. She bolted upright and held her breath as Denny walked in.

"Are you going to let me go?" she asked.

Asclepius set a plate down at the end of the bed and began to slowly shuffle out.

"Let me go home! Please, Denny."

They flinched and turned and looked at her sadly, the downturn of their frown darkening a bruise on their cheek. "I'm not Denny. I'm sorry I lied to you. I have orders."

A wrangled cry of despair forced its way up Helen's throat, and she choked back the following sob. "Please. I didn't realize what I was getting myself into. I'm sorry."

A look full of hurt flickered over their face as they turned back to her. "You really don't know why you're here, do you?"

Helen shook her head, wringing her fingers together. They looked over their shoulder before swinging the door behind them and walking toward Helen.

"This isn't you, Hel. William dug himself a deep hole. You're just collateral in this game between gods and mortals."

Helen shook her head, refusing to believe it. "You're not a god. I would have known."

"I am. My name is Asclepius. I'm truly sorry, if I had any choice, you wouldn't be here."

Helen's tears stung her cheeks as she gazed at them. "I know William owes money. I can pay."

Asclepius reached out to take Helen's hand, and she flinched back. Their arm fell awkwardly to their side, and they sighed. "It's worse now, Helen. William tried to kill Don before he disappeared. He's branded your family."

Helen looked up in shock. William was violent, but not that violent. Right? Asclepius gave her a sad look and turned to leave again.

"Wait! How long will I be here?"

The god shrugged. "Until William comes to pay his debt."

Helen's jaw dropped. "But—" Her plea was cut off by the door slamming. Shit. They didn't know William was dead. He was never going to come. Was she going to die here? She began to sob helplessly. She'd never see her girl again.

35

Spades was a fifteen-minute walk from her house, and June took it quickly. Henry had argued with her, insisting that he should drive her or come with, but he finally listened to her insistence to go alone. She couldn't explain it, but as much as she liked Henry, they had really only known each other a short time, and he had worked for Don up until the day before. She didn't quite trust him yet.

So now she walked down the road, armed with nothing but the hope that her power would work in an emergency. Her mind was racing. What would she do if her mother was there? What if Poseidon was? She turned her face to the sky as she reached a corner and studied the dark-gray clouds floating above.

"Hey, Zeus, if that was you, any help would be great," she whispered.

She received no response, but a small raindrop fell on her cheek. Then another, and another, until it was properly sprinkling. She yanked the collar of her coat up, grumbled about gods and storms, and wrapped her scarf around her head to protect her hair from the rain. The last thing she needed was for her curls to come out of their smoothing gel.

She stepped up to the building that used to be Spades. The windows were boarded, and the sign out front was decayed, so it read SP DE. She took a step closer to read a sign hanging on the door and was hit with a wave of dizziness. It felt different than what was normal lately, more like if someone had taken the powerful air around Athena and magnified it. She fought past the wave of sickness and stepped closer. The feeling intensified, and she moved again. As soon as she was close enough to the door to press her nose against it, the sick feeling disappeared, and she looked up, confused. The sign was gone, and the paint was refreshed. It looked like a set of brand-new double doors. She turned and looked back at the street, which appeared the same.

She quickly backed up, and three steps took her through the odd heavy air that made her feel like falling over. From farther back on the street, the door looked as it did when she first approached. A wooden plank was nailed sideways over it, with a sign pinned up that she couldn't read. The paint was more than half chipped off, and she felt generally uninterested in going in.

She pushed herself back through again, stopping in front of the door. She laughed lightly as the dizziness faded and her mission came to the forefront of her mind. Whatever the strange wall was—because she was sure it was a wall and that it was magic—it must have been meant to deter humans. She was definitely in the right place.

She tried the door, and it swung open easily. As she stepped in, fifty pairs of eyes turned on her. She pushed her sunglasses up on her head, and the men scattered about the club, hastily turning back to their games and conversations. She swung the door shut right as a familiar black car pulled up. She smiled before turning to look around the dimly lit room. She was shocked at what she saw. The window did not look boarded up from the inside. In fact, the street outside was crystal clear and bustling with people. It was as if the window wasn't there. Plush red carpet lined the floor and was covered in an array of rugs. The walls were made of richly colored oak, and sturdy wooden tables were scattered about, surrounded by men playing card games. A large bar sat near the back of the room, decorated with forgotten scotch glasses. The right side of the club held bookshelves, and the left a stage, with two beautiful women swaying to music and singing atop it.

June ignored the questions popping into her head, deciding to chalk it up to gods, and wove her way through the table maze toward the bar. She slid onto a stool and tapped the counter. "Gin rickey, please."

The bartender's face flushed, and his expression flickered between discomfort and confusion. "I'm sorry, ma'am, but we aren't allowed to serve women here."

June bolstered her confidence as much as possible and lowered her face to peer at him over her glasses. "Please don't make me repeat myself . . . or do something worse." Electricity crackled between them for a moment before she straightened up again.

The bartender bobbed his head and began working. "Right away then, miss."

She turned on her stool while he poured gin and lime juice together, and she scanned the bar. She watched the women on stage for a moment, taking in the strange air around them. There were seats at the bottom of the stage full of more men, seemingly awestruck and sucked into their pull. June shook her head, trying to clear the fog that they caused. Some sort of sirens, it seemed. Their voices were haunting and beautiful. They wore silvery dresses and turned in time to the music together, the lights of the bar glinting off every sequin on their dress. She thought it was strange that women would sing in a gentleman's club if they couldn't be served here. As she looked closer, she noticed their dresses were actually thin enough to see through. She made out their undergarments, and a blush rose to her cheeks, forcing her to look away. That made more sense.

When she blinked and looked up again, she noticed that many of the men at the tables were staring at her with malice in their eyes. As soon as she looked at each man, they turned back to their game in turn, but they seemed stiff, as if they were waiting for something.

Except for one. An older man sat near the bookshelves. June faltered as she recognized him; she was sure it was Zeus. There seemed to be static in the air around him, and his amber suit reminded her of sunlight. She hadn't realized how muscular he was before and how ancient he appeared. As the bartender slid a glass toward her, she leaned in to ask, "Who is that gentleman there?"

The bartender shook his head. "Not sure. He came in for the first time yesterday at open, and he didn't leave until close. Same thing again today. Apparently, he was sent by the heiress of something to wait."

June nodded. Eris kept her word, she thought. It was clear she had expected June to follow through. For what reason, she couldn't fathom. She carefully stood and walked toward him, trying to make herself appear larger than she was so the men peppered around the club wouldn't stare again.

She sat on the ottoman across from the stranger, setting her drink on a small accent table to his left. She decided that if Eris sent him, he should know what was going on.

"Hello, I believe you have something for me?" She smiled politely, and the man grinned and shook his head.

"No, ma'am, I can't say that I do."

A flicker of frustration passed over her face before she composed herself and leaned in so she was barely an inch away. "Look, I don't know if you know me, but I know you. And I know who sent you. I'm looking for a man named Don. Don Whittaker. You may know him as Poseidon."

The man in amber looked uneasy as he wriggled in his seat a bit. He looked around the room for a moment before jerking his head down in a nod you would only see if you were looking for it.

"This place isn't safe," he whispered. He reached into the drawer next to him and pulled out a scrap of paper, which he shoved into her hand, mumbling something about not enjoying being down with mortals. She smiled at him and stood, gingerly picking up her drink and striding back toward the bar. She slipped the paper into her pocket and left the untouched gin on the counter. When she turned and pulled her hand from her pocket, a large man grabbed her.

She was thrown to the ground, and her arms were held out on either side of her while a third suit put a knee to her chest and knocked the breath out of her. She opened her mouth to scream, and a handkerchief was stuffed in. Her mind flashed back to the night in the alley, and all her rage and sadness and terror balled up in her chest. She began to thrash around and managed to knee the man on top of her between the legs. He rolled off with a groan, gripping his manhood and curling into a ball. She swung her leg wide around, skirt flying up, and kicked at the figure to her right. Her foot connected with his shin, and he roared in pain, loosening his grip enough for her to yank her hand free and tear the sunglasses from her face. She rolled and stood, looking the last man holding her in the eye. He let go as panic lit up his face and he began to turn to stone.

June scrambled up as more men jumped from their seats and moved to join the fray. She managed to duck out of the way as one swung his meaty fist toward her. She heard it connect with bone as she wove through two tables. Confusion was making them dangerous, and a few pulled out switch-blades or picked up glasses to throw. The women on stage began to sing louder, and June's heart raced in time to the music. Men lunged at her from every direction. It took all her focus to dodge and weave between them. One suit caught her by the shoulder and tore the thin fabric of her dress, and she turned and glared at him, stopping him in his tracks. He went gray, the bit of light-blue cotton still in his outstretched hand. June only watched for long enough to see one of his friends knock him down, causing his head to snap off and spin across the floor. She turned back to face the door and ran. The singers reached a crescendo in their song, and the harmony bore through June's brain, urging her to turn to them.

She clapped her hands to her ears and tried to focus on the door ahead.

As she neared it, a small mousy-looking man that couldn't be much older than her stepped in front, blocking the way completely. She skidded to a stop and glared at him, but he looked up at the ceiling. A demented laugh erupted from his mouth, sounding like it belonged to a much larger body, and his face contorted. June stepped back, and a second later, his chest burst open. His pin-striped suit dropped to the floor in shreds, and she felt someone bump into her as she watched the man's skin turn in on itself. Terror set into her body as wings unfurled from his now bright-red feathered shoulder blades, and four bright-orange eyes took the place of his previous two blue ones, set around a massive black beak. The feathers stopped at his collarbone, giving way to taut red skin thinly covering a mass of muscle. June's eyes tracked to its feet, and her stomach flipped at the large scaly talons now digging into the carpet.

She stood rooted in place as the gryphon threw its arms down and roared loud enough to shake the chandelier above her.

"June!" someone yelled from her side, and she was thrown sideways as the glass light fell, shattering on top of two suits that had lunged for her. The sound cracked around her, and small pieces of crystal and filament flew through the air. June crashed to the ground as terrifying howls and tearing sounds filled the room around her. She caught herself on her hands, wincing as she stood, and blood bloomed under embedded pieces of glass in her palm. She looked around and saw Henry a few feet away.

It took a moment to register that he was yelling "RUN!" over the din of singing, monstrous cries, and glass breaking. She bolted after him, turning to watch as more ten-foot-tall creatures climbed from their human skins around the room. Henry yanked her by the wrist and pulled her between tables and chairs, around the men still sitting in front of the siren-like singers in a daze. The pair turned to face the onslaught of monsters, and as they clambered over each other to reach them, June yelled, "We have to go!"

She took a step forward before turning to Henry and realizing he was staring up at the women. She reached out and yanked on his arm, but he didn't budge. A furtive glance behind them warned her that she had only moments to run before the gryphons would reach them.

She quickly reached over her shoulder and yanked a bit of her sleeve off that was already torn, shredding it into two small scraps in desperation. She reached up and shoved a piece into each of Henry's ears before grabbing his hand and bolting between two suits stuck in their trance. Thankfully, he followed her this time.

As they ran around the right side of the bar, the terrifying creatures lunged after them. Henry jumped over an overturned chair, landed in front of the door easily, and threw it open. June pushed through the wall of magic and out to the sidewalk behind him, where he stopped and bent over, resting his hands on his knees while panting. June watched as the flying red creatures pounded into the wall, toppling over each other. She stared at each one of them, and three turned to stone in front of her. She fell to the ground then, exhausted.

Henry was behind her as she sat, bracing his hands under her arms.

"Come on, June, we have to move." As he said it, she saw the magic waver, glimpsing a bit of the polished door before it returned to a clear image of an abandoned building. She half stood, watching as a man in a suit pushed past the creatures and through the wall. The moment his foot touched the sidewalk, Henry and June ran again. They moved as fast as possible, both gasping for air. They took sharp corners and weaved around pedestrians that threw them dirty looks before they finally slowed to a trot near June's apartment. Henry stopped and looked around, and June placed her hands on her hips, wincing and breathing heavily. How they got out of there alive, she had no idea.

Henry finally caught his breath and asked, "What was all that?"

June grabbed the stitch in her side and screwed up her face. "Gryphons. They're Poseidon's protection."

"Well, what happened? Was he there?" Henry pressed.

June remembered the paper in her pocket and unfurled it, holding it out to him. "No, but I think I may have seen Zeus."

"Trust no one. Times Square at noon," he read, and his jaw dropped. "We have to go!" he exclaimed.

She shook her head. "I think it means tomorrow."

He nodded and motioned to the front door. June stopped halfway up the stairs, frowning. "Henry, what were you doing there?"

He had a sheepish look on his face and shrugged. "I thought you might need help. I was worried."

June pursed her lips and stopped in front of the door. "I think I need to rest, actually." A long beat passed before Henry scrubbed his face and sighed. "I can scope it out, at the least."

36

June rubbed the back of her neck and entered her apartment, anxiety pricking her spine, but as she rounded the corner to her living room, she stopped dead in her tracks. The couch cushions were on the floor, the pictures on her wall were knocked askew, and muddy boot prints decorated her rug. Her heart rate sped up, and she reached for a bat by the doorway, raising it and poising to swing as she walked through to the kitchen. Her apartment looked to be in a similar state as her mother's house was after the suits had ransacked it.

Her teakettle was in the middle of the kitchen floor, handle gone. The tins that normally held her sugar and flour were missing their lids, and nearly every cabinet was open. She set the bat down once she was sure no one was there and looked over the dining room. Her notebook was missing, as was a small jar that housed her savings.

She swore. Of course they would come and take what they wanted.

A bang sounded through the ceiling above her, and she froze, moving slowly to grab the bat again.

A moment later, footsteps pounded near the top of the stairs, and she crept up the first few steps to look around the corner. More creaking from above her echoed through the hallway, and when she peeked around the wall, she saw one of the gray-suited men standing on the top landing.

"What do you want?" she asked, trying to make her voice sound angry, but she was sure there was a squeak in it.

"Here to collect you and William." He grunted and stepped forward. June dodged his arm as he reached out to grab her, and she sidestepped into the kitchen.

"Oh, you want my dad?" She turned and ran through the kitchen, grabbing the door-frame to swing herself up the step. When she reached the bottom, she yanked a heavy piece of William's remains from where it had been tucked on a shelf and turned.

"Here he is—Hey, Dad, meet one of the idiots trying to take me."

June heaved it as hard as she could at the man in the suit. He looked surprised as it spun toward him, hitting him square in the nose. He threw his hands up to his face. June ran straight toward him then, reaching up to ball her fist around his tie and pull him down before he could recover himself. She held him, hunched over, and looked him in the eye.

Once he was stone, it took a moment to loosen her hand from the wrinkled gray she'd grabbed on to—the marble had formed around her fingers. She yanked hard and freed her hand, and she laughed at the mark in the statue. She looked at her nails, and her laugh faded at the gray dust under them. Her mind raced as she imagined scratching someone's skin and pulling it with her hands. Bile rose in her throat, and she shook her head to try and clear the image.

If Poseidon wanted both of them to show up, then they would. Grabbing a scarf from the coat hook, she began digging through the rest of the rubble she'd tucked away until she found a large chunk of his face. It only held part of his eye, his cheek, and the right side of his mouth, but it would be enough.

She gingerly traced a finger down his cheek and whispered, "I'm sorry, William." She set it next to one of his hands and wrapped both pieces tightly in the scarf, then tucked them into her pocket. She stood and wiped a tear from her cheek and closed her eyes, focusing on the outside of the gallery.

Use your fear.

The air thrummed around her, and she clenched her eyes tighter, imagining the smell of the road outside and the coil of fear in her stomach. It had rained earlier, so she knew it would hold the smell of wet dirt and grass, and there would be a mild breeze. She remembered the terror that gripped her when she was chased by suits. She didn't open her eyes until she felt the cool air on her cheeks and found herself outside the diner door.

37

June materialized on Forty-Second Street, with the sun shining brightly above her. She peeked around the corner and could see the decrepit building that Poseidon was hiding in. She grimaced and turned back around, patting her pockets to make sure the pieces of her father were still there. She checked her watch to see it was ten in the morning, and smiled. That slip of paper had said noon, so maybe she would catch him by surprise. She breathed deeply and turned the corner, pulling her forgotten sunglasses from the neck of her dress and slipping them onto her face. She stopped for a moment, briefly considering waiting for Henry, but shook her head. She would be fine on her own.

Approaching the invisible wall took more willpower than she thought she had. Sickness came over her as she took a step in, and all the bad memories she held deep in her mind surged up.

Another step, and bile bit at her tongue.

Another step, and dizziness overtook her.

She clenched her teeth and forced herself forward, thinking of her mother who had been held captive, and Henry. Oh, Henry, how she hoped he was truly on her side.

One final step, and she came out of the haze. She stopped once she was clear of the wall and bent down, retching up stomach acid. It took a few minutes to recover herself, and once she stopped heaving, she stood and shot the shimmery air a dirty look. How could an invisible mist cause more pain each time she passed through? She righted her dress and looked at the building in front of her.

This place really felt abandoned. Bits of the walls were crumbled, and every window seemed to be coated in a thick layer of grime. There was no sign of life anywhere, save for two rats sniffing a puddle of some murky substance under a broken pipe to her right. She took a step forward, and they scurried off.

She kept walking. Halfway to the building, she watched three suits step out from the front door. They looked like the same ones from the factory. All three moved in uniform, pacing in front of the door. They didn't seem to notice her yet, so she quickly looked around, spotted a stack of disposed tires, and ran to duck behind them. She was already exhausted, how was she going to get through them? She wasn't even sure when she'd last slept. The days had morphed together.

She forced herself to breathe and steady her heart rate. It would be okay. Maybe she could distract them somehow. She patted her skirt down and realized that she didn't have anything with her to use, and there was nothing around her either. She didn't want to have to turn them all at once if she didn't have to, then face Don immediately after. Gods knew what else was waiting for her before she even reached him. She could only see one option—to try and separate them. She'd run up and get them to chase her in order to break them apart so she could turn them one by one, like at the bar. Maybe she could even lead one back through the mist wall.

She crept from her hiding place and looked up. The suits continued to pace. She bolstered herself and walked toward them with purpose. Twenty feet away, they still didn't look at her. Ten feet.

"Hey!" she yelled.

The three stopped together and turned sharply. She stopped walking, and they all stared at each other. She took a step forward, and the one in the middle smiled as the other two moved to flank him. Their suits began to bubble. June stepped back. Oh no.

The ties around their necks turned a deep shade of brown, and their bodies began melting together. Their suits grew into massive scales the size of dinner plates, and they rose until they stood at least fifteen feet tall. June took another step back, heart pounding. Three sets of eyes stared down at her, set on top of pointed heads. A low hissy growl started deep in the creature's chest. She stepped back again. The creature's three tongues flicked out, and a bit of green venom dripped from the one on the left, forcing her to stumble back. The drop of venom fell to the ground where her feet had been and sizzled in the mud, causing a rancid-smelling puff of smoke to rise.

Air whooshed out of her lungs as she looked into the middle head's eyes, and she realized that she was staring up into the face of a hydra.

"Stand down." She tried to project her voice as much as possible.

The massive three-headed reptile opened its center mouth and let out a deafening roar that shook the ground beneath them before it whipped all three of its heads down to look at her. Her mind raced as she tried to remember what hydras could do. It had been years since she'd read a story about one in school.

In a panic, June reached up and pulled her glasses off to look into its eyes. The center head froze and let out a pained sound as the stone chased itself across its neck. In mere seconds, the large, hellish monster's head was white marble. She grinned triumphantly as she turned her gaze to the one on the left. As the gray wash started turning the scales of its jaw, the center stump of a neck began to tremble. June stepped back and dove behind a pile of broken pallets as a spurt of green goo shot into the air and showered over where she had just been standing. She looked down at her dress and swore at the fabric that was eaten through by a splash of the stuff. She peeked up over the pile of wood and nearly choked from shock.

Where the center head had broken off, two scaly vines were lurching up through the stone. Bile rose in her throat as more venom spewed and two heads regrew in its place, faster than even her marble could run its course.

She swore again as she realized the same was happening to the other head on the right, and in mere seconds, the creature had five long necks, and all sets of eyes turned on her hiding place.

With a hiss, the head on the left reared up, its neck swelling, before it shot a stream of goo at her. She ran as hard as she could, narrowly avoiding the acidic slime that fell behind her. She threw herself behind another pile of tires and tried to catch her breath, huffing heavily with a hand on her chest. Stone was not going to work on this thing if it was going to regrow heads. She looked around and spotted a long, broken pipe a few feet away.

A quick glance behind her showed the monster pacing. It turned back toward the door, and she sprung up. She whipped the pipe upward, grunting at its weight, and threw herself into a run toward the creature. As she reached it, a tail swept toward her, and she jumped, tripping over her feet and falling to the ground. Stars blinked into her vision and her heart caught in her throat as the creature began shrinking and turned toward her. As its tail wrapped around itself and six arms sprung out of its chest, she leaped forward, thrusting the rusty end of the pipe into it.

The creature let out a shriek loud enough to rattle the windows in the building, and she shoved the pipe in farther, throwing all her weight against it. All five sets of eyes turned down on her, and she glared up, catching each one and watching the marble race up its necks as purple blood spurted from its chest. A drip of venom fell from the head on her right, and she screamed and fell back as it burned her eye.

She scrambled across the ground backward with a hand slapped to her face and tears prickling her other eye, trying to keep it open to watch as the scaly necks writhed around and threw themselves sideways, unbalanced on half-turned human legs.

The creature continued to scream as June crawled to a puddle of water to the left. She scooped some of the muddy substance into her hand and threw it at her eye, biting her scream back as she gasped. The pain was unlike anything she'd ever experienced, and she kept trying to wash out the venom until it faded to a dull thud.

The sounds of thrashing stopped behind her, and her shoulders shook as she turned. She tried to open the eye that had taken the venom to it and bit her tongue at the effort it took. She covered her good eye, and choked back a cry. June couldn't see anything. The world was dark through her right eye, and she tried to hold back a sob as she opened her left and took in the destruction in front of her.

The bottom half of the hydra was slack, with four human legs sprouted around the two scaled ones. Black blood coated its entire body, and her eyes trailed up the rest of it. Two of its human arms were missing, and the rest were stone, which had also captured all five of its heads. They were twisted at odd angles, sharp teeth glinting white in the sunlight, and June's fingers shook as she raised them to her face.

She'd felt the power surge up in her from turning the hydra, and now that it was gone, she felt empty and more tired than before. She braced her hands on her knees, allowing herself a moment to rest before standing and walking around the half-stone, clearly dead, monster.

She slid the glasses back on and made her way through the main entrance quickly. She was thoroughly exhausted, but knew she had to keep moving.

Two staircases stood on either side of the main room, and the whole area seemed to be larger than her apartment. The floor was half concrete, half wood peppered with dents and burn marks. Sconces hung on the walls, some nearly falling off, and she noticed that the staircases were falling apart as well. She approached the one on the left and was shocked to see that nearly every other step was missing, and burn marks decorated the wall that held a railing. She wasn't sure if there had been a fire here or if a fire-breathing creature had come through. She wouldn't be surprised by the latter anymore.

As she lifted her foot to climb a step, she spotted a door near the back of the room and went that way instead. She listened at it once again, and upon hearing nothing, she pushed it open.

Her jaw dropped as she stepped into the small room. The walls looked like obsidian—the same deep black that caged Chaos. Purple light danced around her as candles placed in each corner reflected off the dark glassy surfaces. In the center of the room stood a round table. It came up to her waist and held a small silver bowl on it. She stepped forward and looked in.

The bowl appeared to hold water. As she lowered her face to look closer, the liquid rippled. She squinted and began to see images form. Shapes warped and swam until she could see a clear picture of Henry standing with Poseidon. They looked as if they were having a lively conversation. Henry mimed shooting a gun, and Poseidon roared with laughter. What was this? The image shifted, and it was her mother, lying in bed with Asclepius. The water form of Helen snuggled in to the god's chest, and they seemed to wink up at June. She wrinkled her nose, mildly grossed out, and the image warped again. This time, she had to squint and look closer. As she moved, the image in the bowl did too. She realized that it was her, from the back. She watched as someone stepped forward, holding a gun, and pointed it at her back. The hand in the image cocked the revolver, and she heard a click behind her. She slowly lifted herself up.

"Well, well, June. What do we have here?" Eris' sickeningly sweet voice filled the room.

June turned slowly and grimaced. Eris was standing in the doorway, pistol in hand, legs shoulder-width apart, pointing the barrel at June's face. Eris flicked the tip of the gun toward the bowl, and June flinched.

"What's going on there?"

June glanced down and back up again. The image still showed the gun being pointed at her. "I'm honestly not sure. I'd say the water is showing me the future, but maybe not." She stepped back an inch. Eris kept the weapon trained on her. "What are you doing here, Eris?"

The goddess stepped closer. "Why don't you tell me that? Why are you lurking in an abandoned building?"

June tried to step back again, and Eris shook her head. "If you must know, I'm looking for my mother. Don took her."

Eris lowered her gun. "I thought you were working with him for a moment. I'm looking for a way out of his captivity."

June breathed a sigh of relief and asked, "What do you mean?"

Eris shook her head as she tucked the firearm into the back of her slacks. "Doesn't matter. How were you able to see anything in that?"

She motioned at the bowl of water, and June shrugged. "Can't you?"

Eris shook her head and stepped up to the bowl, bracing both hands on either side and glaring into the surface. "Only Poseidon or his descendants can. Even though Apollo is the God of Prophecy, ol' Donny boy wanted a bit of it for himself. He had this crafted so he could glimpse the future. I've been told it's only partially useful. Sometimes it shows the past, but otherwise it's like having your own little oracle." She stroked the rim of the bowl, and a cold feeling dropped into June's stomach. The mention of an oracle again made her feel sick. If she had any doubts about the father of her child, they would have been gone with this interaction. Not only was the child in her Poseidon's, which would likely give her the same abilities, but Typhon was also sure it had the gift of prophecy. She sighed and then froze as a banging noise from outside the room sounded.

Eris motioned at June and hissed, "Hide!"

June obeyed, ducking under the table-cloth and holding her breath. She moved to cover her watch and muffle it's ticking, but her finger grazed broken glass, and she inhaled sharply. The golden watch had been shattered by the hydra, and the face no longer moved. June raised her hand to stifle her cry instead.

She could see Eris' shadow through the thin fabric, and she hoped no one could see her.

Eris took her weapon out once again and left the room. Dead silence rang in June's ears as she waited. Suddenly she heard Eris exhale loudly. "You scared me, Don! I was just doing a search—" Her voice was cut off, and she emitted a choking sound.

"You're a snake. Even more so than Asclepius. I know you helped that little brat out, and you're trying to leave me for Typhon. You really had the nerve to turn up here after ignoring my call for days?"

Eris choked again, and June swallowed back her cry as tears pricked the corner of her eyes. Poseidon threw Eris down, and

June watched as her shadow fell to the ground in the middle of the large room. She could see the hulking outline of Poseidon step over the woman, and June bit her hand to keep quiet.

"You've fulfilled your use. Take a message up to Zeus for me. I'm done playing games. He will step down or I will kill every one of his agents. I've found a way around his walls. It won't be just here, but in the void."

Eris whimpered. A flash of light made June wince, and the loud bang of a gunshot echoed around. Don held his position with his weapon still pointed at Eris for a moment before stepping back. June couldn't see anything but the outline of Eris' body for five long, quiet breaths.

Suddenly Poseidon's outline appeared in the doorframe. June flinched and squeezed her hand tighter around her own mouth. The god ambled in and placed his hands on top of the table, causing it to shake.

"Little pond, show me the future." His voice sounded strangely affectionate, as if he cared for the porcelain dish, and all the traces of its normal roughness were gone.

June held her breath as Poseidon stood mere inches from her. He began laughing, and she shook as cold terror seeped into her bones.

"Yes, that's right. She will be caught. Show me when she will come here." The water splashed a bit, and his laugh faded. "That's not right."

June watched as he stepped back and turned, peeking out through the door, before turning back to the bowl. "Stupid thing. Get it together." He slammed his hand down next to it, making the table shake and the water splash. He turned, grumbling, and began to close the door behind him. June caught a few of his words before the door closed with a click. "Here, now? Ridiculous. And Henry?"

She stayed frozen in place and listened to his heavy footsteps fade. She waited for the count of sixty before climbing out from her hiding place and glancing at the bowl. The image of Henry running from suits was spinning in the water. He ran into the building she stood in, yanked open the door, and gave her a hug. Then the image reset. June shook her head and turned to the door.

She breathed deeply for another minute before reaching out to turn the handle. It stopped halfway in its arc and wouldn't move anymore. She pushed on the door. It didn't budge. Her heart raced as she pushed and turned and tried to get it to move. Her tears returned, and she turned her back to the entrance, sliding down to the floor. She was scared to make too much noise, but it was clear that Poseidon had locked her in.

38

A long table had been erected in the Great Hall of Olympus, and most Olympians had cleared out. Spread across the table was a map with figures that represented mortals moving about, and Zeus let out a disappointed sigh.

Typhon, standing to his left, glanced over at him, and fidgeted with his hands, before looking back down. A small figure that looked a bit like June was advancing toward a section of the map that was obscured. A large figure blocked the entrance to the blacked-out building, and he watched with bated breath as it knocked her down before she returned the attack.

"I could go down and help," Typhon murmured.

Zeus said nothing, and Typhon looked up from the table to the other gods who had joined their meeting.

Apollo met his gaze with cool regard, but Artemis' eyes held some pity; she worked closely with so many mortals that she had to understand his feelings about June.

Athena's seat was empty, as was Hermes', Aphrodite's, and Hestia's. He looked to Ares for some backup, searching his face for some show of support, but Ares' gaze was distant and bored.

"Zeus," Typhon said, turning fully. "You can't expect her to succeed. She needs help."

"We can't interfere with the mortals," Zeus responded flatly, eyes still fixed on the map.

"I understand the principle, but I've been with her through her whole life. What's one more day?"

"It is the most important day. The day that will change the trajectory of all realms. You cannot intervene."

"She needs me."

Ares finally looked up and spoke. "Your concerns are valid, Typhon, but perhaps we just watch how this plays out."

Typhon glared at him before Zeus turned away from the table and placed a hand on his shoulder.

"Athena caused enough trouble. If I catch you leaving, Hestia will bring you back here, and you will also stand trial. And I can promise you that it will not be nearly as merciful as Athena's was. You will join the rest of the titans." Zeus' stormy eyes lit up as his gaze bore through Typhon, who swallowed. "Do you understand?"

Typhon nodded.

"Good," Zeus said before turning back to the table.

Apollo pointed to the figure that represented June, and the image flickered before growing larger. "What's happening there?"

The group watched in silence as she was joined by another figure, then her image disappeared.

"It's time," Zeus said with a clap of his hands.

39

Hours passed. June knew it by the way her stomach grumbled and her bladder swelled against her undergarments. She desperately needed a bathroom, a hot meal, and a cup of coffee to combat the swimming in her head.

Since the room had no windows, she had no other way to track the time aside from the alarm bells her body set off. Even the candles gave her no indication, somehow still burning at the same level as when she walked in. She sighed and stood, touching her watch face. Maybe she should scream for help? But what if the wrong type came? No, best to stay quiet. If the bowl was to be trusted, Henry would be coming. She walked to the silver bowl and peered down. The same image was still looping around.

"When is it going to happen?" she asked aloud.

The water stopped and began to move the image backward. June rolled her eyes. Maybe Poseidon was right and it was on the fritz. A wave of nausea rose, and she placed a hand on her stomach. A thought struck her. She leaned down close and whispered into the bowl.

"Show me our future."

The water stopped again before it began to swirl. It moved faster and faster, splashing up the sides of its container as it went. June became dizzy from watching and blinked, trying to right herself. Her eyes crossed, and she suddenly fell sideways, the world going black as she hit the floor.

When she opened her eyes, she was in a hospital bed. Sweat drenched her brow, and a doctor swam into focus next to her.

"Breathe, breathe, and push!" he exclaimed.

June's body seized, and her stomach clenched as she pushed down. She suddenly realized where she was—in labor. She looked to the side and didn't see Henry. Her heart sank. The doctor made her push twice more while a nurse held her hand, and she gasped between contractions. Her mind was telling her she was in pain, but if she focused, she could tell that she actually couldn't feel anything. It was a strange experience. She pushed again, and the doctor yelled, "Congratulations!"

The room around her was still out of focus, and she blinked to try and clear the fuzziness. She watched as the doctor raised something up into the air and smacked it. The thing glowed like a small sun, almost too bright to look at. It hit her then. Her child. A piercing scream erupted from it as the doctor began to lower it into a blanket held by a nurse. The babe screamed louder, and the doctor's hands released it, turning to stone inches from the bundle. The gray wash moved up his arms quickly, and a look of panic flickered across his face just before it froze. As the marble reached the top of his head, it began to crumble. Starting at his crown and moving downward, just as quickly as he'd frozen, he turned to dust.

June's hands shook as she raised one, reaching to warn the nurse that held the child. It was too late. As she placed the bundle on June's lap, she was gone, frozen in time for a split second before crumbling to dust, her remains mixing with the doctor's. June looked down at the infant, barely registering the pink hat, and began to cry.

"June? June!"

A voice pierced her eardrums, and a hand yanked the back of her neck. The hospital room she was lying in moved away from her, or rather, she was pulled from it by the collar of her dress. She watched as the image faded, dark taking over instead. Moments later, she gasped as water splashed around her. The inky blackness she'd moved through faded, and she blinked and sputtered as the obsidian room came back into focus. She raised her head and looked up to see Henry holding her.

She threw her arms around him and sobbed. "You came!"

He gave her a tight squeeze before pulling her away, concern obvious on his face.

"What were you doing? You could have drowned!"

She looked down and realized her hair and blouse were soaked in water from the bowl. The surface of what was left in the container was still, but water speckled the cloth around it. She shook her head. "I think I fell over. I'm not sure."

Henry jerked his chin down and looked behind him. June breathed a sigh of relief as she noticed the door was open.

"We have to move quickly," he said.

Before they could move, a voice boomed out on the other side of the door. "Henry! I'm glad to see you," Poseidon said. "Come, we're meeting upstairs."

She grasped his hand, but he shoved her arm away and turned through the door. He glanced back with wide eyes before snapping the door shut behind him, leaving her alone. Panic gripped her.

What was Poseidon going to do to Henry?

Her heart raced as his and Poseidon's footsteps receded, and she waited to the count of twenty before trying the handle again.

"Thank the gods," June whispered, as the door swung open. Swallowing hard, she turned and moved to the left staircase, careful to avoid Eris' body.

Her nose wrinkled of its own volition as she crept up the steps. The smell of decay hit her like a bus, and she had to fight past a wave of nausea when it worsened on the next step. She slid over to the right of the stairs and clenched the rail as hard as possible, praying they didn't collapse and fighting to keep her breath steady and ignore the smell of rot as she climbed.

There was nothing but an empty table on the second floor.

Near the top of the second staircase, she caught the faint whisper of voices above her. She looked up but couldn't make out what they were saying. She crept up the last few steps and came out on yet another empty level, and she stopped. Her heart was pounding, with blood rushing in her ears. One more staircase to climb.

She rounded the corner and began her final ascent. On the fourth step, she dropped to her hands and knees and crawled. The metal edge of the steps bit into the palms of her hands, but she ignored it. Five more steps. Three. She stopped at the top. A thin two-foot-wide wall separated her and the men talking on the other side. Her ears perked up as she made out Henry's voice. Suddenly Poseidon roared with laughter.

Her mind flashed back to the vision in the bowl. Heat rose in her body, and her anger surged up. How dare that *disgusting* god laugh at anything. How dare he even feel the right to smile after the terrible things he'd done.

"Yeah, boys, not too long now and we'll have a proper place. Henry just gave us the contacts through the department to fix us up nice."

June faltered at hearing Poseidon's voice.

"How'd you manage to snag this goofball anyway? Seems a bit useless in my opinion." A loud slamming sound reverberated through the air following the stranger's question.

"We don't talk about our friends that way, James. And Henry here simply got an offer he couldn't refuse, isn't that right?" Silence fell before Poseidon laughed.

The hair on the back of her neck stood on end, and she breathed a sigh of relief. He wasn't against her. A chorus of laughter from the other side of the wall followed Poseidon's statement, and June clenched her jaw. Steeling herself for what was coming, she stepped into the room. She cleared her throat, and silence fell.

"Hello, gentlemen."

Poseidon sat at the head of a large table, with five suits around the rest of the table. The undeniable back of Henry's head was facing her, and he stiffened when she spoke. She tried to send a silent thought to him. It's okay.

The man farthest to the left jumped up and yelled, "Oi! Who let the broad in?"

Poseidon laughed and clapped his hands together, standing with a flourish. He faltered as he looked past her, and his hands dropped.

"Where is William?"

June smirked and stepped forward until she was a few feet in front of the table. She fished the bundle of cloth from her pocket, tossing it to Poseidon. He nearly fumbled the package, and she watched with narrowed eyes while he unwrapped it.

"What is this?" The pieces fell to the table with a clatter.

"You asked for me to bring my father."

Poseidon looked June up and down. "Grab her." He punctuated his words with a snap, and the suit who had insulted her ran around the table.

As he moved toward her, she stepped forward, tearing the glasses from her face and fixing her intense gaze on him. He stopped mid-step and toppled. His shoulder cracked under the weight of his stone body with a loud crunching sound. His face was contorted into a scream that didn't escape.

"I ain't no broad." June sneered at the dead man and looked up at the rest of the group, fixing her glasses again. The tension in the room was suffocating, and she took another step forward. She spread her arms. "So, who wants to go next?"

All at once, the remaining suits shot up. Henry scrambled to the side of the room as chairs scraped the ground loudly, a couple falling with a loud thud. Plumes of dust rose around the men's feet as they bolted around the table. The man to the far right reached June first. He swung his fist hard toward her, and she swiveled, tearing the glasses off her face with one hand and throwing her other behind her for momentum.

The pair locked eyes, and the man fell forward, shattering into pieces. June turned back in time to see the man to Poseidon's left pull out a gun. The last one leaped over the table, reaching for her. His face turned stark white, and he fell through the rickety wood with a loud crash. Splinters and fine dust filled the air, and the cocking sound of a pistol turned June to the last man. He pointed the gun at her, legs braced firmly, and she smirked. She stepped forward and stared into his eyes. He slammed his own shut a second too late, as the marble raced its way up his legs. He froze with his finger on the trigger. June looked down and slid her glasses back on. Her muscles ached, but she felt incredible. Power coursed through her as she stepped up to the remains of the table and looked at Poseidon, who had stood statue-still during the chaos and was looking at her with a strange expression. She couldn't tell if it was fear or confusion, or both.

"Sit down, Don."

He didn't move. She looked to the left of the room, spotting another wooden table, this one long and thin. Atop it was an engraved decanter and six empty whiskey glasses. She smiled, blinked, and appeared next to the table. Out of the corner of her eye, she saw Poseidon reach for his holster, and she *tsked* turning fully to face him. She pointed at the seat behind him.

"I said *sit*." He raised his hands and obeyed, lowering himself slowly. She glanced at Henry, who stood frozen amid a pile of rubble, and jerked her head. "Go find my mother, please."

He dipped his chin, terror etched on his face, and ran from the room.

June turned back to the decanter and popped the top off, pouring herself a generous glassful.

Poseidon breathed heavily. "What are you?"

June turned, swirling her glass. "Your creation, *Don*."

His face drained of color as he watched her.

"Do you know why I'm here?" Silence filled the room around them as she fixed the stopper again. "I'll tell you. It's not because you asked me. I'm not sure if you noticed, but I came at my own time, of my own free will."

Poseidon scoffed. "You're here because I summoned you. I don't know what game you're playing, girl, but I'm owed a life."

June took a long drink, letting the bitter alcohol burn its way down her throat and spread warmth through her chest and stomach as it went. She walked up to Poseidon and dropped the glass over the remains of the table. It fell and shattered, the brown liquid mixing with white dust to create a puddle among the woodchips.

"You have a life there." She nodded to the half of William's face still clutched in Poseidon's hand. "I'd say our family's debt is settled, wouldn't you?"

Poseidon shook his head, amusement playing on his lips. "No, because *I* didn't take it. I don't know what you think you are, or who, or if you're trying to play gods. If you think you hold some power over me, but what I say in this city goes. And the debt is most definitely not settled. Your father owed me thousands as well."

"Well, Donny boy, you're not getting that money back. I'm not sure if it's clicked for you yet, but *I* killed my father. Don't think I won't do the same to *you*."

Poseidon began to stand, and June snatched the marble back from him, slamming it down onto his leg and hissing, "Sit down."

She braced her hand on the arm of his chair and lowered herself to be eye level with him. "I'm actually not here about the debt. I'm here to tell you a story. Don't worry, it won't take long, and it will answer your questions."

She straightened and grinned at him before stepping away and beginning to pace.

"Once upon a time, there was a cute little restaurant in New York. In that restaurant, a girl worked hard every day. She was fresh out of school with big plans to become an artist! She wanted to be famous and make something of herself. She worked her tail off saving for college, which was to begin soon." She paused and looked at Poseidon, but his expression was unreadable. "One day, a handsome man strode in. His presence captivated her, as did his grandeur stories. His words charmed her and made her believe she was about to experience true love for the first time. He made her trust him. Little did she know, he was there to hurt her."

June stopped her pacing and turned to face him. His knuckles were white from gripping the chair arms. He began to stand, and June let a bit of air hiss between her teeth before she reached down, broke off a piece of one of his lackeys, and threw it as hard as possible at him. He dodged at the last second, and she nodded to the chair. With bewilderment on his face, he sat again.

"You see, she skipped her break that day *just* to chat with this wonderful man. He seemed kind, and interesting. Unfortunately, before the girl knew it, he attacked her."

June walked up to Poseidon and braced her arms on either side of him once more. Her voice dropped to a whisper. "That man shoved her down and had his way with her, tearing her in half and breaking her soul. Do you know who that man was, Don?"

He shook his head, as if denying it could make it less true.

"It was you." She let go of the chair and strode away, walking to the only statue standing and circling him. She inspected his face as she spoke. "Then, believe it or not, you had the audacity to come for my mother, because hurting me to get back at William wasn't enough. So, I'm here to settle things. You came to me for a debt. I'm here to collect what you took from me." She leaned on the frozen man. "What you may not have known is that your crime led to me attaining the wonderful gift of turning pigs like you into debris like that." She spat the words at him and spread her arms out, motioning to the rubble around them.

Gods, she hoped he couldn't see through her bluff.

Poseidon opened his mouth to speak, and June raised a finger to shush him. "I understand how badly you wanted me back then. I want you just as badly now. And luckily for both of us, you'll be with me forever. I've been looking for the perfect piece to stand outside my gallery, you see."

June stepped forward, and Poseidon flinched. She moved behind him, tracing her fingers along his shoulder and down his torso. She worked his gun free from its holster and breathed hot air into his ear as she whispered, "I don't like how these look in stone." She rounded the chair to face him again.

"I didn't—" His sentence was cut off by a sharp slap to the face.

"Tsk, tsk, Poseidon. Don't try to lie. You don't think I remember our meeting since? You thought I didn't have the power to stop you." She blinked and shifted to the other side of the room. "Joke's on you. I have help." She shifted back in front of him.

His face contorted, and he tried to rise. She shoved him back down and held her free hand on his shoulder.

She met his eyes and stopped. Was she really going to throw this god into Chaos? She remembered the terrifying monsters it held, and her heart skipped a beat. *Yes, he deserves it,* she reminded herself.

His face was a mask of terror. He clearly didn't know what exactly she was or that she couldn't really hurt him. Not in the way he expected anyway. She grinned and straightened.

"I'll actually give you a choice, as I'm feeling benevolent. Zeus would like a word with you. I'll take you to Olympus and let you face him, instead of decorating my garden."

Poseidon's teeth clenched, and he stood, shoving June to the side. "I can get to Olympus on my own," he spat.

June cocked her head. "Can you? Last I heard, you had a life-ban from the city."

He wiped his hand over his face and suddenly lunged at her. June dove away, holding her foot out to trip him. He stumbled past and swore as he caught himself on a broken fragment of table.

June was behind him in an instant, pointing the gun at his back.

He laughed lightly and tried to turn, but she shoved the barrel against his suit harder.

"I'll make a deal with you, Juniper. I'll go willingly to my death if you'll forgive me," he said.

She pushed away from him and swore under her breath. She couldn't trust this god. And forgive? He was insane. Poseidon rose behind her, and she turned to face him. He still towered over her, but he somehow seemed smaller than before. He was smiling at her, and something inside June snapped. She whipped around, raising her leg and kicking him in the chest, screaming. He fell to the ground on his back, surprise taking over his features.

"I will NEVER forgive you!" Her voice bounced off the crumbling walls of the room, and he flinched. She planted her feet on either side of his body.

As she reached down to touch his temple, his thick fingers wrapped around her ankles. She slammed her eyes shut, picturing Chaos. Poseidon's grip tightened, and the air around them trembled for a moment. As all went still, she opened her eyes to see the void a foot away from them.

Poseidon looked around, eyes frantic, before yelling. As the word "No!" left him, a tentacle reached out from Chaos, stretching toward them.

Suddenly the ground shook, and hot electricity zipped through June. She gasped and blinked, and when her eyes opened again, they were back in the room of the abandoned building.

A wave of dizziness took over, and she stumbled back, accidentally giving Poseidon the space he needed to scramble up.

Her vision finally cleared, and she looked up to see him grinning.

"Bastard," she spat. "What was that?"

He laughed maniacally and stepped toward her. "I'm banned from Olympus, remember?" He reached for the holster on his hip and paused.

Hot rage burned through June. She was not going to let him leave this room. Her mind went blank as cold anger seeped through every nerve of her body. She was sure her hands were shaking as she cocked the gun, mind devoid of any thoughts.

"You were weak then and you're weak now," Poseidon taunted.

That was all she needed. One last reason.

She lifted the sight to her good eye, and pulled the trigger.

The shot echoed around her, and blood bloomed on Poseidon's forehead. A thin hole sat between his brows. June stood, frozen in place, staring at that spot as seconds ticked by before his body fell to the floor with a loud thud.

40

A pair of hands wrapped around June, causing her to flinch. They pried the gun from her hands in the next moment.

"It's okay," Henry whispered.

She breathed out and relaxed. She felt all her emotions crash down on her, and she sagged into Henry's chest and began crying. She sobbed loud and hard as her anger dissipated and grief took its place. She'd just shot him. She messed up the plan.

She felt Helen's tender hands on her arms then and collapsed with her mother, falling into her lap.

"Mom!"

She cried. She tried to force out words, but they escaped her lips in wet gargled bursts, and her mother stroked her hair while Henry rubbed her back. They comforted her for a long while until loud whistles sounded from nearby. The sound grew until it was right outside the building, and June sniffed, sitting up and wiping her tears away.

She looked up at Helen and hiccupped. "I didn't think I'd get you back," she whispered.

Helen squeezed her hand in response, and Henry cleared his throat.

"We should probably go. I'm sure those are the police. The wall is probably down since he's gone."

June nodded and stood, taking both their hands. She had her family back. It would be okay.

"Did he take anything? Money from home or the deed?"

Helen hesitated, but Henry shook his head. "I searched, but it seems he really was just after William."

June nodded and placed a hand on each of their shoulders. "Brace yourselves," she warned before turning, whisking them all away.

June shifted the three of them to Helen's house, although she misjudged slightly, and they landed short of the first porch step. She turned and grimaced at seeing that her mother's face looked a bit green. She hooked her arm through Helen's and led her inside, with Henry following close behind.

June flopped on the couch, running her hands over her head. She let out a loud sigh as Helen situated herself on the chair opposite and Henry sat next to her, draping his arm behind her shoulders. She scrubbed her face with her hands, mind running through everything that had happened. As her hands fell from her face, Helen gasped loudly, and June's head snapped up.

"What? What's wrong?"

Helen jumped up and rushed to June, falling on her knees and taking her face in her hands. "Oh, honey . . . your eye!"

June's hand flew up to where the hydra had burned her, and she grimaced. She'd forgotten about it in the rush after facing the creature.

"Oh, gods. What am I going to do?" she moaned.

Helen *tsked* and rose. "I'll grab a cloth."

June placed her head in her hands as Henry ran a hand up and down her back. She had no idea what she must look like now. She closed her good eye and tried to peek through her fingers, but quickly realized that she couldn't see through that eye. And gods knew what that acidic saliva had done to her skin. It had burned like all hell, though the adrenaline from facing Poseidon had since kept the pain away.

"Let me see," Henry said.

His voice broke her train of thought and she groaned. "No."

"Please, June. I'm sure it's not that bad."

She let out a sigh and raised her face. A flicker of emotion passed over Henry's features for a moment, and he touched a finger to her cheek before the corner of his mouth tugged up in a smile.

"You're still gorgeous. It'll be okay."

June sucked on her bottom lip a moment and nodded. There wasn't much that could be done anyway. Helen rushed back around the corner then and gently pressed a warm cloth to June's face, and June smiled her thanks.

"What now?" Helen asked. She was clearly still shaken, her face pale and her fingers trembling as she clasped her hands in her lap.

June shook her head. "I'm not sure. I-I messed up the plan."

Helen gave her a confused look, and Henry squeezed her shoulder reassuringly before she took a deep breath and prepared to explain everything that Helen had missed during her captivity.

Guide to The Five Realms

Asclepius – Demigod of Medicine; Child of Apollo and Coronis (Naiad)

Ares – God of the Spirit of Battle; often Zeus' right-hand man; Husband to Aphrodite

Artemis – Goddess of the Wild; Leader of The Hunters, a group of warriors who have chosen the pack as family

Athena – Goddess of Wisdom

Chaos – A Primordial Deity; the first creator and where Aether was born, holder of the gates of Tartarus (visit www.abdanielsannachi.com/extras for the universe origin story)

Demigod – Biological child of a god and either nymph, monster, or Mortal

God – Creation of the Titans

Gryphon – A creature that was created to guard the underworld, with the body of a lion, wings, and the head of a hawk.

Poseidon stole them from Hades' guard and experimented in combining them with Mortals until they could shift forms

Earth/Mortal Realm – The world on which Mortals live; magically tied to Olympus

Eris – Titan/higher Goddess of Chaos or Discord; created by Chaos, she holds the raw power of the Primordial Chaos, and could be just as powerful, but struggles to control it

Fates – The three sisters that craft the threads of mortal life; Lachesis, Clotho, and Atropos. Clotho spins the yarns, Lachesis sorts the threads and decides when to snip them, and Atropos weaves the cloth of fate

Hades – God of the Dead; Ruler of Underworld

Hephaestus – God of Craft

Hera – Goddess of Marriage, primarily; Wife to Zeus

Hermes – Titan/higher God of Travel, primarily; one of the few gods descended genetically from a line of Titans

Hestia – Goddess of the Hearth and Keeper of Olympus

Nymph – A race of Olympian with many branches of power from woodland to mountain to ocean divinities that all control aspects of Olympus

Oceanid – Nymphs of the freshwater; they preside over the lakes and are related to Nereids

Olympus – Refers to both the full realm of Olympus and the city of Olympus (also sometimes called "The Golden City")

Olympian – Any being that was created in or born on Olympus, or shares genetic material with another Olympian and could survive living in Olympus; i.e., Gods, Demigods, Oceanids, Centaurs, Harpyai, etc.

Oracle – Mortal or Olympian chosen to channel prophecy

Poseidon – God of the Sea; also known as "Don"

Priapus – Demigod of Gardens; Child of Dionysus

Tartarus – A prison created by Chaos for beings of any other realm

Titan – Creation of the Primordials

Titan God – Biological descendant of Titans; normally child of two Titans but sometimes a descendant of a line of Titans

Underworld – The realm of death

Zeus – God of the Sky or Thunder; King of Gods

On the cusp of war with a prophetic child
joining the family, and fate intertwined
with the gods, the adventure is far
from over for the Georgians.

Turn the page for a sneak peek of...

THE
OATH
OF EVE

The Violents Book Two

1

June still had vivid dreams, although none were like when she visited Chaos or Olympus. In fact, she had seen neither since her last encounter to lay out the plan to defeat Poseidon, which had failed quite miserably. Yet, today, she was woken from a dream of Olympus by her water breaking.

In the wee hours of the morning, Henry had helped her gather things to take to the hospital. She'd let her eyes wander over the paintings gifted by her mother that covered their living room, and she'd taken a moment to enjoy the warmth of their kitchen. Theirs. Together.

Even though Henry had purchased this house on his own, together they'd made it into a home through the end of her pregnancy. And once the house had been completely decorated, Henry gifted her with a beautiful engagement ring. They were wed just days earlier.

It hadn't been long before her contractions progressed and pulled her attention away from her reminiscing, but she still couldn't help but think of Typhon as they drove to the hospital.

Her childhood friend had up and vanished. She hadn't heard from him in months. And as Henry helped her waddle through the massive hospital doors, she whispered to the breeze, "Ty, please come."

Labor progressed quickly, and before she knew it, Henry stood to her right, clasping her hand.

"Breathe, June. Breathe. Just one more push!"

The nurse at June's feet echoed the sentiment, and June bore down with all her strength, her scream filling the room.

"Done!" the nurse cried, and the doctor rushed over to take the small pink thing from her.

June smiled weakly and leaned back. Henry clenched June's hand, craning his neck to see past the nurse, before he beamed down at June.

"A girl!" he whispered loudly, voice filled with excitement.

June's smile widened, although she couldn't shake the feeling that something was wrong. This wasn't the vision she'd seen in Poseidon's bowl of prophecy.

She watched warily as the doctor handed the baby to another nurse, who took her to the sink and began to run water for a bath. As the water touched her skin, the infant cried for the first time. The sound shook June to her core and made her want to cry. Thankfully, the scream faded into a quiet burble of sounds after a moment, and June relaxed.

"Evelyn." She turned to look at Henry. "I think we should call her Evelyn."

He smiled and gave her hand a squeeze. She turned her attention back in time to see the doctor remove his gloves. He reached down to touch baby Evelyn, and her tiny fingers grazed his hand. In a split second, the doctor was frozen, stuck into marble with his hand still outstretched to the baby. June sat bolt upright and yelled as pieces of his stone body crumbled off. She stared in horror as the first nurse hurried over to pick up the baby and get her away from the man falling in on himself. She held it to her chest as June stared and Henry covered his mouth.

The newest addition to the Georgian family was like June, but far more powerful.

As June reached out a hand toward the doctor, jaw dropped in shock, a powerful gust of wind threw open the labor ward door. Both June and Henry's heads snapped toward it, and June let out a strangled sound as she tried to move.

"Typhon!"

He was by her in an instant, holding her shoulder so she stayed put. His face was grave, and her wide smile faltered when she noticed fear in his eyes.

"Ty? What's wrong? Where have you been?"

He shook his head sadly and patted June's shoulder once before sweeping toward the nurse. The god placed a hand on the slight woman's shoulder and something in her seemed to change. June watched, confused beyond belief as he leaned in and whispered something in her ear.

"What are you—" June stopped as the woman handed baby Evelyn to Typhon and began to move out of the room. Finally, he turned back to her.

"I'm so sorry, June-bee, but we have to go."

"Go? Go where? Where the hell have you been? And what are you thinking!"

June's fingers began shaking and she held her arms out to take her baby, but Typhon didn't move.

"I'm sorry," he whispered again.

Suddenly, the air around June warped. Everything in her reality seemed to stretch as thin as thread, and in a moment, she was flying through the air. Typhon carried her out of the hospital room window, and she could only turn in time to catch a glimpse of the doctor's stone dust following them before she was thrown upward into a sweeping current of air.

June materialized in the receiving hall of Olympus, standing up. The moment her feet touched the ground, her legs buckled, and a pair of strong hands caught her. She looked up, breathing a sigh of relief as she saw Henry behind her.

It took a moment to orient herself before she finally caught sight of Typhon a few feet away.

"Ty! Give the baby to me. Now."

He shook his head sadly and turned toward a set of twelve pedestals. June recognized them as the same ones that Zeus had sat on with other Olympians the year before. She could barely recall what they had been discussing at the time.

As she looked in the face of the different gods, a lump formed in her throat. All had a grave look, as if an important death had occurred. She tried to squash her rising level of anxiety over the fact that she still hadn't held her child, and she turned her attention to Zeus.

June gathered all the strength she could muster and stepped forward, pointing her finger up at him. "I don't know what you all think you are doing by bringing us here, but I want to leave. Now." She tried her best to keep her tone even and stepped forward again. As she moved, her shaking lessened and she began to feel more normal, as if Olympus itself were lending her energy.

Zeus motioned to Evelyn. "This is the child, the newest Gorgon?"

June opened her mouth to speak, but Henry cleared his throat. "It's—it's actually Georgian. Well, Chekov now."

Zeus raised an eyebrow at him before turning his attention to June. "Well, young one, it seems we have a bit of a situation."

June's face heated. "The only 'situation' is that you cradle-napped my newborn whom I haven't even held yet!"

Zeus held her gaze for a moment before snapping and motioning to Typhon, who walked back to June. He held Evelyn out with an apologetic look, and gently placed her in June's arms. Tears welled in the new mother's eyes as she gazed down at her girl. She was perfect. She had dark hair, like June, but it seemed to be straighter, and her eyes were closed and puffy around the edges. Her cheeks were flushed pink and her bottom lip was pouted out, as if she was about to cry.

Zeus cleared his throat, interrupting June's first moment with her newborn, and she glared at him.

"As you know, you failed to take care of Poseidon. His essence woke on Olympus this morning. We believe he's gone back to New York at this time, but we have no way of knowing if he'll stay there, or what he's up to. We would like you to keep an eye out and intervene if necessary. And then there's the issue of that child."

He motioned to the baby, and June held her protectively. "There is no issue here. She is my child, and she was born less than thirty minutes ago!"

Zeus sighed as if he was tired of the conversation. He glanced at Hera, who had been silently watching.

"As for Poseidon," June said, "perhaps if you'd had the foresight to turn off his exile from Olympus, the plan to throw him into Chaos would have worked! I tried. I really did. But as soon as I got him here, we were thrown out like pieces of paper on the wind. It's not my fault, and not my problem anymore."

June looked around at the other gods, recognizing Apollo, and noticed that all of them looked uneasy.

Hera spoke then. "Juniper . . ." Her voice was kind and warm. "Other issues aside, that baby is Poseidon's. She is immortal and belongs on Olympus. She will grow fast, strong, and powerful. The mortal world is no place to raise her."

"And would we stay here with her then?"

Hera looked uncomfortable as she reached out and held Zeus' hand. "No, dear. Mortals are incapable of surviving for long here. She would stay with us, alone."

June blanched and looked at Typhon helplessly, who was wringing his hands. She swiveled back to Zeus and pointed an accusatory finger at him. "You mean to tell me that you yanked me from a hospital room immediately after labor in order to tell me that you plan to take my child away *and* that her biological father has been set loose on our home city once again? And you want me to take care of him again? You're all *fucking* insane." She spat her last sentence out, and in her peripherals she could see a few gods flinch. She was sure that no one had spoken to Zeus like that in a long time.

He shook his head. "I'm sorry that we took you so suddenly. I'm sure you remember that time passes differently here. It's up to you in the end, Juniper. As you said, she is your child, *but* she is also Poseidon's. Our children have a place here and the community they need to harness their abilities and thrive. Immortals belong on Olympus. She belongs here."

June faltered then, stepping back and turning to Henry. She looked at him, tears threatening to spill over, and he squeezed her arm reassuringly. When he gave her the barest hint of a nod, she spun back to Zeus. "Take us home. Now. We will raise Evelyn there just fine on our own."

Hera raised a finger. "Just to be clear, she will not have the protection that you did. It has been expressly forbidden for any god, or titan, to become companion to man again." She looked pointedly at Typhon, who was staring at his feet.

It dawned on June then. That's why he hadn't been around. He wasn't allowed to. She really thought he'd come back with them . . .

She straightened her shoulders and snapped at Zeus. "Never mind that. I stand by what I said."

She felt Henry move closer behind her and turned to see him nod his head firmly.

Zeus sighed and waved his hand. "Very well."

The world around June's little family dissolved.

About the Author

Ari is a trans author and editor from Oregon. After having his first novel published while living in Australia—a true crime memoir— he quickly dove into writing fantasy. He  spends his free time reading, listening to mythology podcasts, and playing D&D. Follow him on Instagram, Facebook, or TikTok @darkmythauthor to stay up to date. To learn more about him and his books, visit:

www.abdanielsannachi.com